MARKO

BRATVA BLOOD BROTHERS #4

JAX KNIGHT

Marko
Bratva Blood Brothers #4
Copyright © 2024 Jax Knight
Published by Hudson Indie Ink
www.hudsonindieink.com

Marko/Jax Knight – 1st ed.
ISBN-13: 978-1-917448-05-5

PROLOGUE

MARKO ROMINOV

LONDON - THURSDAY MORNING - EARLY MARCH

My eyes drooped as I dozed in my chair, my mind numb from running one tedious report after another for my brother Miki. Tax time was the bane of my existence, especially when it involved hiding the money we laundered among our legitimate businesses. However, at last I was almost done. Just another few minutes should do it and then I could head to bed for a well-deserved rest.

I rubbed the back of my neck as my heavy lids closed and my head bobbed as consciousness slowly ebbed from me.

"Beeeeeep!"

A blaring alarm jolted me upright. I scanned the screens in front of me with a renewed alertness. Finally, there was movement in the bank account I'd been monitoring.

My fingers flew over the keyboard, hacking into the account with growing excitement to match the widening grin on my face.

"Yes!" Fist-bumping the air, I nodded. I knew I was right to keep an eye on it.

Being the leaders of the Bratva in the UK, my family had many enemies, including some we hadn't even known existed. The last couple of years had been a bloody nightmare as we faced one enemy after another. We had finally killed the man who had supposedly been behind everything, late last year.

The few months of quiet since had felt ominous for me, like the calm before a storm. I had never quite believed our problems were over.

That's why I was monitoring this account. It had belonged to Aiden Mathieson, a corrupt lawyer who ran a human trafficking organisation. He was also an enemy who, unbeknown to us, had held a grudge against my family and spent the last couple of years trying to cause trouble for us and our ally, the head of the Polish Mafia, Janusz Glowacki.

Things had started with Mathieson backing an attempt by Glowacki's second, Lev Petrov, to overthrow him. However, the night before Petrov planned on killing the entire Glowacki family, he and two of his co-conspirators, Piotr and Simon Nowack, had gone out partying and abducted, raped, and murdered my sister Krissa.

However, as drugged up as they were on excitement and cocaine, they were careless and left DNA evidence behind and had been caught by the police. That had effectively put an end to their uprising against Glowacki and secured his family's lives, but left a gaping hole in ours.

My gaze flicked to the photograph of Krissa I kept on my desk. Her beautiful smiling face, so full of life, made my heart clench. It was so unfair that such a kind soul had been taken in such an awful way.

"Fuck!" I slammed my fist down hard. I should have protected her better.

Guilt and anger warred for control inside me. My chest felt constricted, and my breathing laboured as I looked at the image of my sister.

Of course, Krissa's death was only the start of things. Via his go-between, another lawyer called Nigel Simpson, Mathieson had also been behind more recent attacks on my family and our businesses and almost caused the death of both my cousin Romi and Glowacki in the process. Not only that, but his cronies had kidnapped my other sister, Sonia. Thankfully, she was okay, but it had brought back terrible memories for my whole family.

Rage boiled inside me, but I forced it down, reminding myself that all the men who had murdered Krissa or caused harm to my family more recently were all dead now. Or so we hoped, provided Mathieson was the last in the long line of enemies, as he claimed when we'd tortured him. However, neither my brothers nor Glowacki and his sons were entirely convinced and not knowing for sure had been eating away at me.

Picking up the photograph of Krissa, I removed the back of the frame, then slipped a knife out of my pocket and flicked it open. Pricking my thumb, I spread the blood over the pad before pressing a bloody fingerprint to the back of Krissa's image.

There were several such prints there, all made with every vow to her to avenge her death. Now, I made a further vow that nobody else would die on my watch. My family had suffered enough, and I was determined to ensure they never had to worry about enemies taking us unaware again, not if I could do anything about it.

After replacing the photo, I returned my knife to my pocket, feeling more in control of my emotions.

My eyes flicked back to the screen, and I hacked into the branch of the bank where the money had been transferred.

Mathieson had kept several secret bank accounts. However, the reason I'd chosen to watch this account was that it had differed from the others. Whereas all his other accounts had been opened under false identities for himself, this one had been created in the name of a woman, Jessica Adams. The difference had made me curious. Hence why I'd set up an alert to tell me if anyone accessed it. And now someone had, and the money had all been transferred elsewhere.

My heart raced as I followed the money trail from the

Jessica Adams account straight into another account under the name of Melissa Martin.

Another woman? Who was she, and what was her connection to Mathieson?

Frustration gnawed at me. Despite my efforts, I had found no link between Jessica Adams and Mathieson. Now, Melissa Martin had entered the picture.

I resumed typing and hacked into the branch where Melissa Martin's account had been opened. After a while, a grin spread across my face as I studied the transaction. A bit more digging and I had enough information to tell Miki.

Unlike Mathieson's other accounts, we hadn't divulged this one to Interpol with the others, choosing instead to monitor it. We didn't want to profit from human trafficking; we might be criminals, but human trafficking was a big no-no for us.

So, we'd made Interpol aware of the money in the others, just keeping this one to ourselves for a reason. If Mathieson had a partner, it was possible this account could lead us to the person. And if it didn't? Well, I still suspected whoever this woman was, she'd be the key to us finding out once and for all if we had anything else to worry about or not.

Excitement surged through me as I raced to Miki's office.

CHAPTER 1
MELISSA MARTIN

LONDON - THURSDAY MORNING – A
SLEEPLESS NIGHT

y neck and shoulders ached from tension, and a headache was forming behind my overtired eyes.

Rubbing the bridge of my nose, I stifled a yawn as I made myself a large coffee.

I'd had a sleepless night, my mind whirling with a mix of emotions in a kaleidoscope of feelings ranging from denial to curiosity and anger to guilt, then back again. All of which were weighed down by a never-ending stream of questions that had my brain working overtime throughout the night, refusing to let me sleep.

Leaning against the kitchen worktop, with droopy eyes, I sniffed my latte, the aroma itself enough to make some of the tension ease from my limbs. Smiling at one of my favourite smells, I sipped the drink, savouring the feel as it slid down my throat, warming me from the inside out.

After fuelling myself with the best nectar known to man, well in my opinion at least, I grabbed a quick shower.

Not willing to go full blown cold water yet, I turned the nob to lukewarm. My pyjamas were tossed aside as I stepped into the cubicle and allowed the water to cascade over me, sighing as it slowly brought my body awake inch by aching inch.

When I finally felt awake enough to go for it, I turned the nob to full cold and squealed as the icy water hit me, making me shiver. It always amazed me that no matter that I knew it was about to get freezing, the change in temperature always shocked the hell out of me, anyway.

A couple of minutes was all I could handle, but at least I felt more alive and clearer headed than the zombie woman who'd got into the shower.

Drying quickly, I put on my usual morning attire of yoga pants and bra top and headed into the living room.

I chugged down a large glass of water with lemon and ginger and then began the next part of my regular morning routine.

My dad was a man of discipline and he had always encouraged me to create a good morning routine, which he said led to a productive day, healthy habits that lasted a lifetime, and an overall happier life.

Grief washed over me in waves, and I closed my eyes. A sob tore from my throat and tears pricked my eyes. Lord, how I missed him. I couldn't believe he was gone.

I could almost hear his voice cutting through my

anguish telling me to *"Hurry up, buttercup, get your exercises done. You've somewhere to be."*

Buttercup had been his pet name for me, and it made me smile. Nodding to his imaginary voice, I did what he said, blinked back my tears, lifted my chin, and moved straight into my warrior pose.

Stretching through my usual yoga poses eased the tension in my shoulders, and I finished with the sun salutation.

I had practised gymnastics as a child and so had always been supple. However, as an adult who no longer took classes, I found that yoga helped me keep that flexibility and fitness I'd enjoyed as a youth.

By the time I finished, my headache had disappeared, and I was glad I hadn't needed to resort to medication to get it to go as I sometimes did.

Next, I sat in the lotus position and let my mind clear further with a short meditation.

Finally, I changed and put on some makeup before picking up the letter that had caused my world to tilt on its axis yesterday and resulted in my sleepless night.

The buzzer rang.

"Yes?" I answered.

"Taxi?" a male voice said.

"Be right down," I replied.

After grabbing my bag, I headed out to meet with the lawyer who held the knowledge his letter had hinted at, my stomach churning with both excited anticipation and the fear of the unknown.

CHAPTER 2
MARKO
THURSDAY MORNING – NEEDING TO KNOCK

"We've got movement on Mathieson's account!" I stated, bursting through Miki's door without knocking.

Aw hell!

Miki and Eilidh were kissing again.

They couldn't keep their hands off each other, and it wasn't the first time I'd interrupted them. It seemed to be my fate these days.

Eilidh had been living with us for the last few months. You would have thought I'd have learned my lesson and remembered to knock by now. Obviously, I hadn't.

At least kissing was all I'd walked in on. The last time was much worse; they were making out on top of the desk, and it was an image I really couldn't get out of my head. I cringed at the thought; I wasn't a voyeur, and I certainly didn't want to see my big brother doing the dirty deed.

These two weren't the only ones either. My sister

Sonia and cousin Romi got married recently and my brother Ash and his new wife Gracie had only returned from their honeymoon a couple of weeks ago. This house was full of couples all getting it on and I was the only single one here. While I was happy for them, it was a bit annoying at times. Embarrassing too.

The other day I walked in on Romi with my sister Sonia in the games room. I would never look at our snooker table the same way again. Plus, I really wanted to purge my eyeballs out with the snooker cue after seeing that.

Seriously, these were not the sort of sights any brother wanted to see. Cringing at the thought, I shook my head and shivered with displeasure. God, I really needed to learn to knock.

"Sorry," I mumbled, as Eilidh jumped off Miki's lap and sat on the desk beside him.

Her face was flushed pink. Obviously as embarrassed as me.

"You were saying?" Miki asked, sounding pissed off at being disturbed, but I ignored it. It wouldn't happen again. I definitely was going to work on knocking, but right now there were more important things to think about.

"The money was transferred from the account Mathieson had set up in the name of Jessica Adams to another account here in London. I hacked into the bank manager's emails and there was one from a family lawyer based here in London, Fitzpatrick & Son, telling him that the transfer was to go into an account in the name of Melissa Martin," I told Miki.

"Another female?" Eilidh asked, and I nodded.

"How is she linked to this Jessica Adams?" she asked again.

"No idea yet."

"Have you looked into this Melissa Martin?" Miki asked.

"Of course. There is only one account of that name at the branch where the money was transferred, and I got her address. I also hacked into Fitzpatrick & Son's and checked the calendar for Mr Jonathan Fitzpatrick, and it seems he had a meeting with her first thing this morning. What do you want me to do?"

"Get Luca and Trigger involved, watch Fitzpatrick and dig into him and also watch her, see what she does and find out who she is and her connection to Mathieson," he said.

"On it!" I clapped my hands together in glee. It had been about six months since we killed Mathieson, and it looked like finally the last bit of the puzzle was about to unfold.

"Tell Trigger to let his guys handle Simpson for now," he added, before grabbing the back of Eilidh's head and kissing her again. Geez!

"God, I'm outta here!" I cried in disgust.

Really? Couldn't he wait until I had left?

"You're just jealous," Miki laughed as I closed the

door and tried hard to block out the sounds of their make-out session all the way back to my office.

Rubbish, I'm not in the least bit jealous!

I scoffed at the notion.

There was no way I was jealous. Why would I be? I was young, free, and single, and enjoyed not being tied down. I hadn't been in a relationship for around eighteen months and was quite happy with that. Ever since I'd broken up with my last girlfriend when I discovered she was cheating on me with her boss, I decided not to get involved with anyone else and to play the field.

It wasn't as if I ever had trouble getting laid. As a young, rich guy, I had my pick of the ladies. They always knew where they stood with me, one-night stands were all I did these days.

The connection all the couples in the house had wasn't something I needed. They could keep their serious relationships and their loved up looks to themselves. No-strings-attached sex when I wanted it suited me just fine.

Yep, keep telling yourself that! The annoying little voice in my head sneered at me.

Tutting at it, I decided not to dwell on what exactly it was trying to tell me and pushed all thought of romance, or my lack thereof, to the back of my mind and turned my thoughts back to the task at hand. Discovering if there were any more enemies hiding in the shadows was far more important than thinking about such nonsense.

After some more digging, I learned that Melissa Martin

was twenty-five years old, so a year younger than me, and studying photography at a local college.

As I looked at her driving licence picture, my breath caught. The woman staring back at me was drop dead gorgeous. With long black hair and bright green eyes, pale skin, and full pouty lips; she was just my type. Very sexy!

What the hell had she to do with that slimeball Mathieson? Surely she wasn't his business partner? Or a lover? Biting my lip, I studied her photo. She looked too young but who knew? Mathieson had swung both ways, and he liked his lovers young, so she could be. The thought sickened me. Why else would she be getting a large sum of money from the bastard, though? Maybe there was another explanation?

Narrowing my eyes, I stared at her picture.

Who are you, beautiful?

As I grabbed my backpack and the gear I'd need; I bit back a smile. Whoever she was and whatever her connection to Mathieson, I'd soon find out.

My heart sped up, but I put it down to adrenaline at the thought of closing in on another potential enemy, and not the fact that I would really like to get to know Miss Martin intimately. If she turned out to be an innocent party, I hoped that getting to know her would be a real pleasure for both of us, but if she turned out to be our enemy, she was in for a whole world of trouble because beauty or not, woman or not, I wouldn't let her threaten the peace my family had just found.

CHAPTER 3
MELISSA

LONDON - THURSDAY – THE
BIOLOGICAL

Leaving Fitzpatrick & Son's office, I clutched the large, padded envelope to my chest, feeling stunned at all I had just learned. As the fresh air hit me, I stopped, unable to go any further. Lost in my thoughts I stood there on the pavement as the bitter wind whipped around my face and neck and I didn't even notice.

It had been less than a year since I lost the man I called dad, but in my hands was a letter from my biological father. I knew very little about him and strangely enough, I had never given him much thought. Until today.

Mathieson. Aiden Mathieson.

The name swirled in my mind. The name of my father. My biological father. Or so Mr Fitzpatrick informed me. Which was strange because that wasn't the name my mum had told me.

My mum said that my biological father was called Simon Hughes, and they had met at school and had a relationship in their final year. They were together for about a year before my mum caught him with another girl a few weeks prior to the end of their last term. Then she discovered that the girl wasn't the first. He had been cheating on her throughout their relationship. It broke her heart. And that's why I'd never wanted to know anything else about him.

Mum hadn't known she was pregnant until a few weeks after they had split up. By then, school was over and he was heading off to university, so she never told him about me, and we had always thought he'd been unaware of my existence. Apparently not.

And yet, he had never contacted me in all these years. I wasn't sure how to feel about that. My brows furrowed and tears sprang to my eyes, and not just from the icy sting of the wind.

Sniffing hard, I pulled the collar of my coat tighter around me with one hand and clutched the envelope with the other. My thoughts were a jumbled mess as I tried to understand what Mr Fitzpatrick had told me. Aiden Mathieson was missing, presumed dead, and that was why he'd contacted me.

Who was this man whose blood ran through my veins and what had happened to him? What had caused him to disappear? Or who? He had obviously changed his name at some point. Why? And did that have anything to do with him going missing? Or was whatever had caused his disappearance something else entirely?

A sense of dread made me shudder. Did I even want to know?

Yes, I had to admit, I did. I was curious to know more. That one question plagued me as I waited in the cold for the taxi to arrive.

Why didn't he ever get in touch?

Even though I had been happy with my real dad, that still hurt. The thought sent a flash of guilt through me, but I pushed it aside. My dad wouldn't have wanted me to feel guilty for being curious about who my biological father was, and curiosity meant nothing. There was nobody who could ever replace the man I loved, who was there for me whenever I needed him, who taught me everything I knew, and who showed me the value of unconditional love.

It was difficult to imagine what life would have been like without him.

When my mum had told her religious parents she was pregnant, they disowned her. Thankfully, her older sister, who was a teacher, took her in and Mum could go to college after my birth and gain some qualifications. She then got a job as cabin crew with British Airways, where she met a charming older man called Oliver Martin. He swept her off her feet.

It was no wonder. He was tall, handsome, rich, and had the air of a refined gentleman. Mum was a beauty with her long black hair and bright green eyes, so she caught his eye immediately. They fell fast and hard and were soulmates. Within a few months of meeting, they were married, and he adopted me. Their relationship was of the type I longed to have myself someday.

Dad's official profession as an arts dealer meant we travelled a lot. We kept an apartment building here in London, but most of the time we lived abroad. It was a great life, and we had lots of money as I grew up. Because of travelling so much, I was mainly home-schooled. My mum had a knack for languages and my dad, well he was exceptionally intelligent and had a knack for everything, so I was very well educated.

Oliver Martin was the best husband and dad anyone could have wished for, and life with him was full of love and excitement. Mum and I had been lucky to have him in our lives.

Sadly, my mum passed away when I was ten from an aneurysm. She collapsed one day with no warning. One minute we were in the garden enjoying the sunshine, the next she was complaining of a headache and within a few minutes, she had collapsed and died.

Dad and I became even closer after that, although neither of us ever got over her loss. And now he was gone, too.

Closing my eyes, a sad smile tugged at the corners of my mouth, and I bit back the tears that threatened as I thought about my parents. God, how I missed them.

"Martin?" a gruff voice called, pulling me from my thoughts.

Turning around, I saw a taxi stopped at the side of the road. The driver said again, "Martin?"

"Yes," I nodded.

As I sat inside the taxi on the way back to my apartment, I peered at my name on the envelope.

Mr Fitzpatrick was not aware of the contents and could only provide me with some basic information about the man he was acting for. He told me he had simply been instructed to give me the envelope six months after Aiden Mathieson's death or disappearance and to transfer money from a bank account, which had been originally set up in my mother's maiden name, to me.

Everything felt surreal. Finding out who my biological dad was had been a bolt out of the blue, after all of these years of not having a clue and frankly not giving a damn. Nevertheless, learning he'd been missing for six months was a huge shock and the size of the legacy he'd left me was an even bigger whammy. I was suddenly a few million pounds richer, but I wasn't sure that any of this had actually sunk in yet.

Tracing the letters on the front of the padded envelope with shaky fingertips, I wondered again what was inside and what sort of man Aiden Mathieson really was. It seemed odd that someone would make plans for the possibility that they might disappear, and that worried me greatly.

Who were you and what were you involved in?

My insides churned, making me feel queasy, and although I couldn't wait to open the envelope, I was also dreading it. I wanted to know what it contained, yet I was suddenly scared to find out. For some reason, I had a genuine fear that the money wasn't my only legacy and that whatever I learned from this envelope was going to change my world forever. And after all the changes that had occurred in my life recently, I wasn't sure I could cope with any more.

———

When I returned home, I spent the day completing an assignment for college and ignoring the envelope, my fear of the unknown overshadowing any curiosity I had about the contents.

Finally, after dinner, I couldn't delay it any longer. My hands shook, and I felt sick with nerves as I tore the envelope open, wishing I hadn't procrastinated for so long, and opened it before I'd eaten.

Inside was a letter and a key.

The letter was cold and the contents very worrying. Frowning, I reread it, not entirely sure exactly what to make of it all.

Melissa,

Mr Fitzpatrick will have told you I am your biological father. Your mother and I had a brief fling in school, but I moved away to university and lost contact with her and of course, later I changed my name. So, even if she had planned on telling me about you, finding me wouldn't have been easy.

As such, I only discovered your existence after your adopted father worked for me several years ago, and I have kept a close eye on you since. If you're reading this, I am either dead or missing, in which case you can assume I am dead.

Either way, my demise will have been at the hand of one of my enemies, and that might even be your uncle. While I admit I was never a good man myself and have done many things you would no doubt find appalling; your uncle is a complete psychopath. Although we share the same father and were business partners, I never trusted or liked him.

Over the years, he manipulated me into dangerous situations but avoided risk himself. He was behind the deaths of my sister Leona and her daughter Clara, who were killed for his associates' amusement. Apart from my parents, they were the only people I have ever cared for in my life. So, after discovering this, I swore to avenge their deaths. That's where you come in.

The key is to a safety deposit box at the branch of the bank where an account has been opened in your name. When you see the contents, you will understand why it is crucial that he is stopped.

You will need to get the evidence to do that. Inside the box is everything you need to know about him so that you can obtain the information required to ensure his downfall. I trust you to handle this because of your inherent morality, which neither I nor any of my associates possess.

Utilise your skills to retrieve this information and pass it to the National Crime Unit. Find a trustworthy contact there that cannot be easily bought off. Your uncle is a prominent figure and will do everything he can to protect himself and his reputation.

The money I sent is to help keep you safe. Although I never knew you, you are my daughter and so, I do not want you to suffer the same fate as Leona and Clara.

I know if anyone can do this, you can. Be cautious. He is a very dangerous man. He should not be underestimated, and if he becomes aware of your existence, he will come *after you on the off chance that you know too much.*

Aiden Mathieson

Disappointment filled me. The letter was impersonal. I wasn't sure what I had expected, but not that. Despite never caring who he was before, I couldn't help but wonder about him now. Oliver Martin would always be my real dad to me, and he was the best, but he was gone now, and it would have been nice to have known how my biological father had felt about me since he was obviously gone now too. However, it didn't seem like he'd felt anything.

Puffing out a breath, I shook my head. I didn't know what to think about this.

My biological father admitted to being a bad person and said my uncle was a psychopath that wanted me to bring down. What the hell had he got me into?

Well, I would not get involved. They could both go to hell. I didn't want any trouble.

However, that night as I lay in bed, sleep eluded me yet again and I lay there thinking about the contents of the letter. My agitation made me restless. My mind was all over the place as I stared into the dark for hours, tossing and turning, unable to calm my thoughts. I was having a hard time processing things.

Who was this uncle of mine and had he really killed his half-sister and her daughter? What kind of person would do that? I didn't know these women, but guilt tugged at me. I really didn't want to be involved in any of this, but if it was true, could I really ignore things and not do anything about it?

"Aargh!"

Frustrated, I flicked the light back on, picked the letter up and read it yet again. The first time I'd read it, my feelings were mixed with hurt and disappointment at how impersonal it was. The second time, I was filled with shock. This time, I was bloody pissed.

"Fucking arsehole!" I scrunched the letter up and threw it across the room.

How dare this man put me in such a dangerous position? Why would he do that?

Of course, I could simply ignore the letter and never open the safety deposit box, like I initially thought. That was what I would prefer to do. After all, I didn't owe the guy anything. But from what the letter said, it looked like I could be in danger whether I went to the bank and opened the safety deposit box or not.

Raking my hand through my hair, I frowned. The air was cool, and I shivered. Rubbing my tired eyes, I climbed back into bed and pulled the covers up around my neck.

Maybe if I went and opened the box, there would be enough information to hand straight over to the authorities and be done with it. I'd let them decide how to proceed. Nodding my head, I decided that was what I would do.

First thing in the morning, I would go to the bank where the money had been transferred and open that bloody box, find out what the hell all of this was about, then pass the information on.

Hopefully, I could hand it all over to the police and forget about it. They could do what they liked about it. That was as far as I was willing to go. I wouldn't put myself in danger to get any further information, no matter what my biological father suggested.

With that decision came relief and I finally relaxed enough to fall asleep.

CHAPTER 4
MARKO
EARLY HOURS OF FRIDAY MORNING –
SURVEILLANCE

Yawning widely, I continued to watch Melissa
Martin's home.

My tired, heavy eyes swept over the house
before me. It was a large and attractive modern property,
split into two apartments. Melissa stayed in the larger one
at the top, while the smaller apartment below was currently
unoccupied.

I'd only managed to do a basic dig into Melissa's
background before I left the house last night, but I had
some of my guys checking things out further. For now,
though, the information I had on her was limited and not
very helpful.

Melissa Martin was the daughter of an art dealer who died
in Monaco about ten months ago. They had been rich prior to
his illness, but after paying medical bills and other debts, there
was little left. Melissa wasn't destitute by anyone's standards,

but her finances had taken a huge hit. Of course, with the sizeable sum of cash that had been transferred into her bank account this morning, I guessed that wasn't the case anymore.

With her dad gone, Miss Martin had obviously not wanted to stay in Monaco by herself and had returned to their London apartment just a couple of weeks ago. She was now attending a local college, doing a photography course. Neither father nor daughter appeared to have had any link to Mathieson. At least none I had found yet. But there had to be one.

A pounding behind my eyes made me wince, and I closed them for a second to give them a rest. As soon as I did, the picture on her license came to mind. Licking my lips, I let the image of her solidify in my mind's eye. Lord, the woman was gorgeous. Those pouty lips called to me, and I wondered what they would feel like against my own. Or wrapped around my cock. The appendage in question jerked in longing at the thought.

Geez, I needed to stop fantasising about a woman who might be an enemy.

My mind bombarded me with the same questions I'd been asking myself all night.

Who are you? What's your connection to Mathieson? And are you a threat?

Annoyed that the answers still eluded me, I huffed out a tired, frustrated breath and rubbed my forehead, trying to ease the ache behind my eyes.

Normally, I would enjoy the challenge it took to find

out the answers to these questions, but tiredness was making me impatient and headachy.

My whole body was stiff from sitting in the one position most of the night. Nothing had happened, and I was so bored, I'd almost drifted off at one point. Luckily, I'd brought a flask of coffee with me and that had kept me awake. However, by the time dawn approached, there was none left, and a few hours later, I was nearly done for and in severe need of some shut eye.

Before the alarm had gone off alerting me to the movement with Mathieson's bank account, I had been working on a personal project and had been too engrossed with it to remember to go to bed. I had a problem that way. Whenever I was busy with work or personal projects, I tended to forget to go to bed and simply grabbed a nap in my office chair when I couldn't stay awake any longer.

As a result, I hadn't had a proper night's sleep in days, and it was taking its toll on me now. I checked my watch and groaned.

Unfortunately, Luca, who was due to take over the surveillance this morning wouldn't be here for at least another few hours. He had a business meeting to attend first thing. So, I pinched my thigh and slapped my cheek to stop my eyes drifting closed while I silently watched the house.

Stretching my arms up over my head, I stifled a groan as my back and neck creaked. God, I could really do with another coffee and maybe a massage right now. Unfortunately, there was no chance of either.

Damn, it had been a long night. I rubbed at the back of my neck and fidgeted as I checked my watch again. It had literally only been a couple of minutes since I'd last checked it and I was about ready to climb the walls.

Police shows always skimmed over surveillance and you never saw just how long and excruciatingly boring doing this kind of thing could be. Or how bloody difficult it was to stay awake when nothing was happening.

Not to mention the fact that I badly needed a pee. I looked at the container I had in my backpack for just such emergencies and frowned in disgust.

Hell no! I need to stretch my legs, anyway.

After checking that the street was empty, I made sure the interior light was turned off in the cab, so it wouldn't draw any unwanted attention if anyone was looking out of a window. Then I silently opened the van door and stepped out. My stiff legs protested at the movement, and I had to bite back a groan. Thankfully, they soon loosened up as I walked on silent feet towards a small park area. Behind the cover of some bushes, I quickly did my business. Relief flooding me as I released myself.

Returning to the van, I settled back into the seat and prepared for another few hours of boredom. Or maybe not. I straightened in the seat. Miss Martin was heading this way.

Hmmm. Where are you off to, sweetheart?

Melissa didn't appear to notice me sitting in one of our nondescript white vans across the street, dressed like your average worker in dark blue overalls and a baseball cap.

She didn't even look my way, but unable to stop myself, I looked at her. Wow, if I thought her beautiful before, well neither her picture nor ogling her from a distance had done her justice. She was even more beautiful in real life.

Since she was on foot, I assumed she was going to walk to wherever she was going or take public transport. Either way, I needed to follow. Underneath my overalls, I had on jeans and a dark T-shirt, so I quickly shucked out of them, grabbed my black hoodie and backpack and hurried after her.

We didn't go far. Around fifteen minutes' walk from her apartment, we turned a corner, and I realised she was headed for the bank where her account was set up. I stayed close on her heels until she entered the bank.

Following her inside, I pretended to read some leaflets on bank loans while I watched her speaking to a member of staff. A couple of minutes later, a man, whom I assumed was the manager, appeared. He greeted her and then led her into his office where they remained for quite a while.

Another member of staff entered the office with what appeared to be paperwork and then left again. A further minute passed and Melissa emerged with the manager, but she didn't turn to leave. Instead, they headed through a security door. Before the door closed, I noticed stairs at the end of a hallway leading down. It looked like they were headed down to where the vault and safety deposit boxes were kept.

Interesting.

Unable to follow her downstairs and unwilling to hang

around inside the small bank any longer in case my actions caused suspicion, I stuffed one leaflet in my pocket and headed back outside to wait.

Spying a coffee kiosk across the street, I made my way over and ordered a badly needed latte. As I took a deep breath of the rich aroma, the fatigue began to lift, and I felt more awake with each inhalation. Taking the first sip, the warm, velvety liquid energised me instantly, spreading a comforting heat through my body and sharpening my senses.

Standing there sipping the drink also helped me look less conspicuous as I watched the door. While I was waiting for my quarry to reappear, I checked in with my assistant Josh. He helped with a lot of my legitimate business but also my less savoury stuff. I'd tasked him with finding out a bit more about Melissa Martin, but because of an issue with one of our legitimate building projects he was working on, he hadn't had the time to do more digging on her yet. So, unfortunately, there was no new information for him to give me.

Just as I finished up my call, Melissa finally reappeared.

CHAPTER 5
MELISSA
FRIDAY MORNING – OPENING PANDORA'S BOX

My guts churned as I walked all the way to the bank on autopilot, buried in my thoughts and feeling jittery, desperate to find out what was inside that damn box.

The bank manager appeared almost immediately after the teller called him and took me into his office. I signed some paperwork, and he handed me a bank card for my new account before taking me downstairs to the vault where the safety deposit boxes were kept.

As the man keyed in the security code to the door, I bit my lip to hide my smirk. It was something I could have opened with my eyes closed. Being down here brought back some bittersweet memories. I had never actually broken into a bank, but I had often broken into personal vaults and safety deposit boxes elsewhere with my dad. I loved those memories, but at the same time, they saddened me. His death was still so new and my grief was still too raw to think of the times we spent together without feeling like I wanted to cry.

Taking a deep breath, I pushed aside my grief. This wasn't the time to break down.

Stepping into the room, I glanced around. The walls were lined with little square compartments, each with a number. I followed the manager over to number 113. My box apparently. After opening the metal door, I removed the box inside.

Once I'd retrieved it, the manager escorted me to a small private area behind a screen which allowed for boxes to be opened away from unwanted scrutiny.

"I'll wait outside," he said before leaving.

My hands shook and my stomach churned even more as I stared at the box for a minute. I had been desperate to open it, but now that I had it in front of me, I was feeling a sense of impending dread.

Did I really want to do this? Hell, no!

Anything to do with my biological dad who confessed to being a bad person, or his psychotic brother, wasn't something I really wanted to know about.

Last night, I'd convinced myself that I could just hand the letter and whatever was in the box over to the police and they could investigate things. Now, however, I wasn't so sure.

Mathieson had mentioned my dad doing a job for him and my unique skills in the letter. That would surely pique their interest. I didn't need any enthusiastic law enforcement officer looking into my past and discovering what types of jobs we had done. Dad was gone now, so it wasn't like it would matter to him anymore, but it very much mattered to me. I had no plans of going to jail for any of my past indiscretions.

But what else could I do? I was alone. How was I expected to deal with all of this?

My head throbbed as I looked around the space, hoping for answers that didn't come.

There really was nothing for it. I simply had to bite the bullet, open the box, and find out where to go from there.

My nerves were fraught. I gingerly lifted the lid up a half inch and stopped, dropping it, as if I expected something to suddenly jump out at me. Chuckling, I shook my head. I knew I was being ridiculous. Yet, why did I feel like I was about to open pandora's box?

God, I really didn't want to do this. The whole thing had me afraid.

I wanted to just walk away and forget all about it. Surely, if I laid low and didn't appear to be a threat, this uncle of mine would leave me alone? Right? Then I'd have nothing to fear. Mathieson had said the guy would come after me if he knew of my existence. But why? If I was not a threat, why would he bother?

Nodding to myself, I was about to return the box unopened, but stopped. I was being a coward, and that was not how my dad had brought me up. I could hear his voice in my head telling me to *"Suck it up, buttercup,"* and *"feel the fear and do it anyway,"* just the way he often did when I was young and in need of a pep talk. So, I took a deep breath and yanked it wide open. The air in my lungs came out in a whoosh and I realised I had been holding my breath.

There was a small white envelope inside with my name on it. My hands shook as I pocketed that to read later, but it was the large, thickly-stuffed brown envelope that drew my immediate attention. I tore it open, knowing that whatever was in there was about to change my life.

The contents spilled out onto the counter, revealing documents and photographs. I picked up the first photo and immediately recognised MP Timothy Evans-Hughes. He was also in the second one, sitting at a table smiling beside a man I now knew was Aiden Mathieson. With them sitting so close together, I could see the family resemblance.

My breath hitched as the shock hit me. My uncle was a famous MP and member of the current government in the UK. Well shit!

As I lay the two photographs to one side, I noticed a document which looked like a template for an email invitation by an event company called *Darkest Desire Productions.* The email logo stated in small print, "*where the darkest desires of your dreams are enacted.*"

It gave a time and place for the attendee to be for collection and advised all necessary items for the event would be provided, along with a reminder that locations would remain anonymous. A warning advised that attendees would suffer severe consequences should they leak any information about the event.

What the hell?

What sort of event was this?

My eyes widened in horror, and I covered my mouth with one hand as I fought back nausea while I quickly rummaged through the rest of the photographs. There were at least twenty, each showing the gruesome aftermath of someone's life. The people in the photos had obviously been murdered violently. There were a lot of women and several men, most of whom looked like they had been butchered. All the females were naked, unlike the majority of the males. Dear god!

There was one last photograph showing Evans-Hughes and three other men standing over a dead male, wearing hunting gear, their knives dripping with blood. Oh shit! The MP was a murderer. No wonder Mathieson said he was a psycho.

Double checking the envelope, I found a small dictaphone still inside, and played it. It was a recorded conversation between two men, whom I quickly realised were Mathieson and Evans-Hughes. Mathieson asked when the next hunt was set for. Evans-Hughes was annoyed and told him not to discuss these things on the phone but then gave the date: Saturday 12 July at the Island at 7 pm. I had a terrible feeling about this.

While I listened, I flipped over all the photographs, feeling sicker by the minute. Each had dates and places on the back, some saying The Estate, some The Island, and others saying Cazar, Ibiza. I glanced at the photograph for the 12 July, and the dead man in that picture was the same as the one in the picture with Evans-Hughes and the three men.

Oh, hell no! I realised what this was; it was a company creating events, or more correctly hunts, for people to fulfil their darkest desires in reality. Hence the name, I supposed. Horror filled me. Breathing deeply through my nose, I gulped back the bile that rose in my throat. This was a snuff company providing people to be murdered as entertainment for others.

Holy shit! I was in trouble.

My heart filled with dread as I came to the understanding that not only was the MP, my uncle, involved in this horrifying activity, but it seemed that he might be the one running things. Mathieson was right, my uncle was a real psychopath. And he wanted me to take this man down? What the fuck?

My breath quickened, my heart racing as panic rose in my chest. My vision blurred, and I swayed as sweat broke out all over my body. Grabbing the wall to steady myself, I dragged air deep into my lungs as I tried desperately to calm down.

Finally, my breathing returned to normal, and I bit back the fear that had threatened to consume me.

Shit, I needed to get out of here, take time to regroup, and think about my next move. But first, I needed to secure this information. My dad's training in caution kicked in, and I quickly used my phone to snap pictures of everything in the box before loading the contents into my bag and forwarding all the pictures to my email.

After quickly closing the box, I put it away, then hurried outside.

"Everything okay, Miss Martin?" the manager asked.

"Yes, thanks," I forced out as my head swam and my vision blurred again. I needed fresh air, fast.

Hurrying up the stairs, I said a quick goodbye and practically ran for the door, my stomach threatening to give up its contents with every step.

As soon as I was outside, I closed my eyes and took a deep breath, then turned towards home, thoughts swirling in my head as the images from the photographs assaulted my mind.

CHAPTER 6
MARKO

FRIDAY MORNING – MEETING LITTLE
MISS POUTY LIPS

t felt like forever before Melissa Martin finally left
the bank, and she immediately turned towards home,
looking a bit distracted.

Glad we were on the move again, I continued to
shadow her from across the road, staying out of sight. We
were about halfway to her home, on a quieter residential
street, when I realised I wasn't the only one following her.
A tall, muscular man in a dark jacket with the hood drawn
up was quickly approaching from behind.

Shit! The hairs on the back of my neck stood on end, a
primal instinct warning me of imminent danger.

"Fuck!" I muttered as I watched helplessly from the
other side of the road, unable to cross for the traffic.

What the hell was he up to?

A stream of cars blocked my path, and a van obscured
my view. So, I didn't see him reach for her until it was too
late.

As the guy grabbed her bag, Melissa tried to hold on to it, but he yanked it out of her hands, roughly pushing her down on the ground before he ran off.

"Hey!" she shouted, trying to get up.

As soon as there was a break in the traffic, I darted across the road and straight to her.

"Are you okay?" I asked, offering my hand to help her up.

When Melissa stood, I noticed how petite she was. Looking down at her small hand in my larger one, I was hit by a sudden feeling of rightness.

"That guy stole my bag!" she cried, pointing to where the man was now climbing onto the back of a motorbike with another guy. The driver sped off with the culprit and her bag.

"Shit!" she cried again, seeing them disappearing along the road.

Narrowing my eyes, I watched them go. Huffing a breath, I turned back to Melissa.

The men might have escaped for now, but hopefully not for long. I'd hack the security footage in the area and see what I could find out about that bike and the occupants later.

Meanwhile, I realised this was my opportunity to get to know Miss Martin.

"Are you okay?" I asked again. "Did he hurt you?"

"No, I'm fine, but I had some important information in that bag. Damn!" she said.

Little Miss Pouty Lips looked visibly shaken, her

hands trembling slightly when I suggested calling the police. I couldn't help but notice the uncertainty flickering in her eyes as she hesitated, before finally nodding in agreement. That second of hesitation piqued my interest, and I wondered what had prompted it.

Once the call was made, I guided Melissa into a nearby coffee shop. The warmth and aroma enveloped us as we entered, offering a brief respite from the tension outside. I bought her a coffee, hoping it would provide some comfort. Then we settled at a table by the window, where we could keep watch for the police.

"Thanks, and sorry about this. I guess I'm keeping you back from whatever your plans were."

"Not at all. I didn't have any plans that were important," I told her. "I'm Marko, by the way. Marko Rominov," I said, finally realising I hadn't introduced myself yet.

There was no point in giving a false name. If she was involved with Mathieson, she might have recognised me, anyway. When the police came, I would give a witness statement, and she would find out my name then anyhow. Besides, it was an excellent test of her reaction.

I watched her intently as I reached my hand out towards her to shake. She took it, with no sign of recognition in her eyes. Good! I couldn't help my overwhelming feeling of relief at that.

"Melissa Martin. Thank you for stopping to check on me and calling the police," she replied with a smile, which took my breath away.

"No problem. Hopefully, they will be here soon, and you can report the robbery. I'm just sorry that I wasn't there in time to actually do anything to stop it," I told her, and I meant it.

"Yes, there was something I wanted to pass on to someone else, something important," she replied cryptically, biting her bottom lip. I stared at it, totally distracted by those full, pouty lips. "And of course, there was my purse and ID and my new bank card," she continued, and I mentally shook my head and tuned back in.

"While we are waiting for the police, why don't you call your bank and make sure the card is stopped, and another one issued?" I suggested.

Melissa nodded and did that while I sipped my coffee, pondering on who had grabbed her bag and why. I couldn't help the feeling in my gut telling me it had something to do with Mathieson.

Afterwards, we chatted for a while about everyday things. Melissa's eyes sparkled as she spoke about her college course and her recent return to the UK.

"My dad passed away less than a year ago," she said, her voice tinged with sadness. "I moved back here after living abroad for a while. My mum passed away a long time ago, and I don't have any siblings, so it's just me now."

Melissa's openness made me believe she wasn't hiding anything, and there was nothing in her demeanour to suggest any nefarious intentions. Despite this, I couldn't shake the feeling that she had to be connected to Mathieson somehow.

While she talked, my attention kept drifting to her full lips, imagining all the things I would like to do with them. Her eyes, a gorgeous shade of green, were so expressive that I felt I could get lost in them. I wondered what they would look like partially closed in lust. The thought made me shift uncomfortably in my seat, and I forced myself to think of other things, trying hard to deflate the semi that was making its presence known in the confines of my jeans. Thankfully, I had just got it under control when the police arrived, and we had to give our statements.

When we were done, I insisted on walking her home, and was happy to get the chance to continue chatting with her. As we approached her apartment building, she seemed awkward, and I knew the feeling. There was tension between us, and it was definitely of the sexual variety, or at least it was for me.

"Melissa. I realise we didn't meet under the best of circumstances, but I really enjoyed talking to you and I would like to see you again. If you want to?" I asked tentatively.

"I'd love to." She grinned.

Hell yes! I mentally high-fived myself, grinning widely.

The slight blush rising in her cheeks was sexy as hell and made me think that this attraction wasn't all one sided.

"Give me your phone and I'll pop my number in."

Little Miss Pouty Lips eagerly handed it over, and my

grin widened at her enthusiasm. Once I'd input it, I sent myself a text.

"And now I have yours," I told her, handing it back.

As I did so, my fingers brushed hers and the surge of attraction coursing between us took my breath away. My eyes flew to hers and in that moment, it was clear she'd felt it too.

"I'll call you soon to arrange something," I promised, smiling before saying goodbye.

Despite my reservations about her connection to my family's safety, I couldn't deny the enjoyable time we had spent together. I wanted to see her again on a personal level.

"So what the heck?" I thought aloud as I walked away. "I like her, and she seems to like me, too."

Back at the van, Luca was already waiting.

I'd known Luca Orlov all of my life. We grew up together, and he was Miki's best friend. Luca's dad, Stefano, had been my dad's best friend, too, and so Luca's family came to the UK when we did. Stefano returned with his wife to Russia when my parents were killed, but Luca remained here. He ran all of our legitimate entertainment venues because he was loyal and trustworthy, with a natural charm. He was more like another brother to us. As such, he had a room at our estate where he spent a lot of time.

"Any updates?" he asked as I approached.

"Yeah," I replied, filling him in quickly on the robbery and Melissa's safety.

"I'll leave you here to keep watch. I'm taking the SUV."

Luca nodded. "I've got it covered. I'll see you later for the night shift."

With a nod of thanks, I climbed into the driver's seat of Luca's SUV, which was parked behind the van.

As I drove to one of our nearby London apartments for a nap, all I could think about was Melissa. A quick message from Josh told me he'd pulled the security footage from the area where the robbery had taken place and emailed it to me. Unfortunately, he still hadn't found the connection between Melissa and Mathieson yet.

That was annoying, but wouldn't be a problem for long because the next time we met, I decided, I would figure out how to obtain that information from her. In the meantime, I went to bed with a smile on my face at the prospect of seeing my Little Miss Pouty Lips again soon.

CHAPTER 7
MELISSA

FRIDAY AFTERNOON/EARLY EVENING –
MARKO, THE SILVER LINING

As I swung open the heavy door to my building, I turned and waved enthusiastically to Marko, a broad grin lighting up my face. That he wanted to see me again filled me with a thrilling mix of anticipation and nerves. Sure, I knew I should steer clear of romantic entanglements until the mess my biological father had dragged me into was sorted. But come on— Marko was undeniably handsome, with a charm that could disarm anyone. And his kindness and quick thinking during the robbery? That sealed the deal. Passing up his offer would have been foolish.

Despite the unsettling events of the day, I ascended the stairs to my apartment with a buoyant step. Once inside, I meticulously checked and secured every lock, my state-of-the-art security system offering some peace of mind. Yet, as my dad and I were all too aware, if someone wanted to get in, they would.

While changing into more comfy clothes, I replayed the harrowing events of the afternoon in my mind. Lost in my thoughts, I had nearly reached home before noticing my surroundings. A sudden, chilling sense of being watched preceded the sharp yank on my bag from behind. I fought to keep my grip, but the thief's forceful shove sent me sprawling, the impact jarring my elbow as I hit the ground. That's when Marko rushed to my rescue.

"Marko Rominov," I whispered to myself, testing the sound of his name on my lips. I liked it. I was sure Rominov was Russian, and I had detected the tiniest trace of a Russian accent when Marko talked. The memory of his voice sent a warm flush to my cheeks, and I couldn't help but smile at the thought of my sexy saviour.

The street hadn't been busy when the robbery happened, but I was glad at least someone had been there when it occurred and I hadn't had to endure the aftermath alone. The entire ordeal had unfolded in mere seconds, leaving me physically unscathed but emotionally rattled.

Unfortunately, there was no way for either of us to chase the thief as he climbed onto the back of a motorbike and sped off. Watching the bastard get away, I felt glad that I had taken photographs of everything and also separated things between my bag and pockets.

The timing of the robbery, just moments after leaving the bank, seemed too perfectly timed to be mere coincidence.

But was it just a random, opportunistic attack by thieves hoping to find some cash from a customer? Or was

I the target because of the information in the safety deposit box? Somehow, I thought the latter was the most likely explanation. Which meant it was the MP.

The MP, that was how I planned on thinking of him, because I never wanted to think of him as my uncle. I refused to claim him as a blood relation, so I would not call him my uncle, and Timothy Evans-Hughes was just too long-winded to keep thinking of him by name, so the MP it was.

A shiver ran down my spine as I realised that meant the MP knew of my existence and suspected my biological father of spilling all of his dirty little secrets to me. And somehow he knew about the box and wanted the contents.

Aw, shit! What the hell was I going to do?

Suddenly, my legs turned to jelly, and a dryness spread through my mouth. Sitting on my bed, I focused on drawing in slow, deep breaths.

With my head in my hands, I mulled over my options. There really wasn't any choice. The MP needed to be stopped and my plan to simply pass the information I had to the authorities would not work.

Even if I sent the stuff to Interpol anonymously, there was just not enough evidence. A man in the MP's position could easily make a few incriminating photographs and a voice recording disappear. In fact, that was obviously what he tried to do by having my bag snatched, which was why I had mentioned nothing to the police who took my statement, as I knew it was likely pointless.

My stomach twisted into a tight knot of nerves.

The robber had only taken my bag this time, but I wondered what he would do next because I was sure this wouldn't be the end of things. I was in big trouble.

As much as I hated to admit it, I would need to fulfil my biological father's last wish. I was going to have to obtain that additional evidence to guarantee that the MP was sent to prison for a very long time and ensure my safety.

Damn it! Of all the legacies to leave me, why had Mathieson left me with this?

Thank god that he had at least provided me with so much money. To pull off what I would need to do, I was going to need money. And if I couldn't pull it off, well, I just might end up needing to go into hiding. Not something I wanted to do, but at least something my dad had prepared me for.

"Aargh!" I screamed, pissed off that the new life I was creating could be ended so soon.

Just when I met Marko, too. Sadness swept over me at the thought of never seeing him again. We'd only just met, but I knew already that he was special and someone I wanted to get to know better.

The very thought of the man had me smiling again. I was so glad that he had walked me home. I really hadn't relished the idea of walking back alone and I'd thoroughly enjoyed spending the extra time with him, which led to him asking to see me again. Hopefully, we would spend more time in each other's company soon. I couldn't wait.

Another of Dad's sayings was 'every cloud has a silver lining'.

"Yep, Dad, you were right, every cloud and all that," I said out loud, chuckling to myself and hoping that wherever he was, he could somehow hear me.

And what a silver lining Marko was. Phew! I mean the guy was hot with a capital H. Around six-foot-three inches of muscled perfection with the most beautiful grey eyes I had ever seen. Very sexy. And smart. I smiled, thinking about how easy he had been to talk to. And his voice gave me goosebumps, especially when that sexy Russian accent peeked through.

Sighing heavily, I bit my lip as a wicked grin spread over my face. Was there anything not sexy about the man?

I had been amused when he told me he worked in IT for his family business. He talked about it with such enthusiasm, his entire face lighting up. He was a geek, a total nerd by the sounds of things, but one who looked like a God.

Wow, a sexy nerd. Brawn and brains. Definitely my type. Yep, I was into him. I doubted many women could resist such a sexy specimen. A sudden rush of heat headed south, making me squirm. All this thinking of him was making me really horny, but now wasn't the time for that. I had serious business to take care of.

A sigh escaped me. I really didn't want to do this, but avoiding it wasn't an option anymore; I had to face this head-on. Gathering all the remaining items and grabbing my phone, a glass, and a bottle of wine—surely necessary

—I settled onto my bed. The letter from Mathieson and the memory stick awaited. Half an hour later, the bottle was half empty, and my mind spun with thoughts.

Holy shit, the MP was a fucking psycho! Mathieson hadn't been lying about that. His letter gave me the MP's address and told me more about the sick goings-on in the world of *Darkest Desire Productions*. Just as I had thought from the photographs I had seen, the letter and memory stick confirmed that the company did indeed cater to mega-rich people who wanted to pay to carry out their darkest desires, usually in the form of hunting down and murdering people, often with rape and torture involved.

The sheer cruelty of finding something like that entertaining seemed unfathomable. The thought that there were many sick individuals out there willing to pay money to inflict such acts on others was utterly horrifying. These people had to be stopped, and the company shut down. However, I wished fervently that I wasn't the one tasked with this responsibility.

My shoulders sagged as the feeling of being completely out of my depth weighed heavily on me, compounded by the loneliness of it all. How the hell was I going to do this on my own?

Mathieson had really landed me in it. I bloody hated the bastard for that and from now on I vowed I would not recognise him as my biological father. He wasn't and never would be entitled to be called father by me. He was simply a sperm donor. My dad was the only father I had and the only one I ever needed. Mathieson could rot in hell. White-hot anger fizzled through my veins, and I paced the room unable to sit still. Picking up a cushion, I held it to my face and screamed into it until my throat felt raw. How could that bastard put me in danger like this?

Why couldn't Mathieson have just sent this stuff to the Police? Or paid someone else to get the information for him and then pass it to the police? Why did he have to ask me, the daughter he'd never met, to do it? I knew I had certain skills, but I was just a young woman on my own. Surely he could have found another person, or more likely several persons, more suitable?

But he didn't. He chose me. Now, whether or not I liked it, I was in deep.

"Suck it up, buttercup," the nagging voice in my head taunted. I sighed, begrudgingly acknowledging its wisdom. There was no use wishing Mathieson hadn't thrown me in at the deep end. That wouldn't change a thing. I was in this now, and my survival depended on completing the mission.

Pouring another glass of wine, I immersed myself in the details of the MP's security setup. Predictably, it was top-of-the-line, befitting a prominent public figure harbouring a scandalous secret. Apparently, he was meticulous and kept detailed files on everything related to his business. That was a definite plus when trying to gather evidence against him. However, accessing his encrypted files required navigating through layers of sophisticated security measures. Then there were several security guards and several bodyguards to deal with, too.

Sitting back, I sipped the rest of my wine while going over all the details again in my head. Between the high-end security and the encoded computer programs involved, it was one hell of a system to crack.

My dad would have relished the challenge and the opportunity to bring such a despicable person to justice. If he were still here, maybe I would have felt the same way. Instead, I felt overwhelmed. I nervously chewed my lip, mulling over various options. It wasn't that I lacked the capability. The issue lay in the complexity of the security system involved—I couldn't possibly execute such a heist alone. I needed help, and that posed a significant problem.

Dad had always worked solo or with me; we trusted no one else in our line of work. I had no contacts suitable for this kind of job. There was no one I knew whom I could enlist for help. I was stuck unless I hired someone, but finding a trustworthy accomplice willing to accept payment for such work was no easy feat and would undoubtedly take time.

I sighed heavily, not relishing the prospect of the daunting task ahead. Nevertheless, it had to be done. Pushing aside my apprehension, I focused on reviewing all the information I had gathered so far.

Once I had enough evidence, I would need to anonymously contact someone at the National Crime Unit. It was crucial to ensure the MP remained oblivious to my involvement. If the police delved too deeply, they might uncover my criminal history, or worse, the MP could engineer it. Neither outcome was desirable, and the thought of ending up in jail terrified me. Since my dad's passing, I had turned over a new leaf, except for this slight detour, and I intended to keep it that way. But how I would manage all of this without exposing my past remained uncertain.

Exhaling deeply, I ran my hand through my hair and rubbed my tired eyes. My mind felt drained. Rest was essential; I couldn't think clearly in my current state. Exhaustion weighed heavily on me, my eyelids drooping with the need for sleep. I resolved to revisit everything the next day, when my mind would hopefully be sharper.

I retrieved my "to go" bag from under the bed, which I always kept packed. Dad ingrained in me the need to be ready to flee if our activities were ever discovered by the police or the criminals he crossed, and I maintained that readiness. It seemed prudent given the current circumstances, so I added the memory stick and my bank card. My passport and another in an alternate name, along with driver's licenses in both names, were already inside.

Before closing it up, I also tucked in the money withdrawn from my account during its activation at the bank, just in case. A foreboding feeling gnawed at me, suggesting I might need it.

With the bag securely back under the bed, I trudged into the bathroom, changed into my pyjamas and brushed my teeth on autopilot. Yawning widely, I climbed into bed, and I'd just got nice and cosy and was dozing off when my mobile rang.

My eyes flew open, and excitement fizzled through me

at the sound because there were so few people with this number, and none would phone me this late at night except the person who had just taken it a short while ago. Marko!

Feeling all gooey inside, I reached out to grab the phone, knocking it clear across the room in my haste.

"Shit!"

Scrambling out of bed, my legs tangled with the duvet, and I went sprawling forward, landing hard on my front and knocking the wind out of me.

"Ooof!"

Panicking that Marko might hang up and I'd lose the chance to hear his gorgeous voice again, I commando crawled towards the phone, grabbing it and flicking the icon to answer.

My heart pounded as I gasped for breath.

"Hi Marko," I said, panting hard.

"Hey there, Melissa, just checking in to see how you are after the events of earlier today?"

That he cared enough to ask gave me a warm fuzzy feeling inside.

"I'm fine thanks," I replied, desperately trying to calm my breathing down.

"So, I was wondering if you still wanted to meet up?"

"Sure," I wheezed.

"Are you sure you are okay? You sound out of breath."

Oh, hell. He's going to think I'm some weird pervert panting down the phone at him. Dragging the air into my lungs, I released it slowly before answering.

"I'm fine. I couldn't sleep so thought I would do a

quick workout to help tire me out," I said, pleased with myself for coming up with a plausible excuse for my breathiness.

"Oh okay. Yeah, I get it. I do that myself sometimes."

God, his voice was dreamy. I could lie here and listen to it all night. Something about it calmed me and yet turned me on at the same time.

Marko cleared his throat, and I realised that there had been complete silence while I was thinking. Shit! What the heck was wrong with me? I was blowing this. Geez, could I get any more awkward?

My face was flaming, and I was glad he wasn't there to see it. I wasn't usually this awkward around men, so I wasn't sure why I was suddenly acting this way with Marko.

Probably because you can't stop thinking about tearing the guy's clothes off and climbing him like a tree! An annoying little voice stated.

"So, would you like to meet up? And if so, when are you free?" he asked again, sounding a little less sure of himself.

"Anytime this weekend is fine with me, actually. I just returned to London a few weeks ago, and apart from attending college, I don't really do anything else at the moment. With no friends here, I certainly don't have a social life either, so I'm pretty much free all the time right now," I said, my words rushing out before I could stop them. Cringing inwardly, I hoped that didn't make me sound pathetic, but it was true.

"Great, how about meeting for a late breakfast in the morning? I have a business meeting first thing near where you live, so I can swing by and pick you up about ten?" he said, and I could hear the smile in his voice.

"Yes. That sounds perfect," I replied, injecting as much enthusiasm into my voice as I could. There was no way I wanted him to think I wasn't interested. The grin on my face and butterflies in my stomach told me just how interested I was. My lady parts were also making their interest known. My nipples were hard and my core wet just from his voice. I couldn't wait to see him again and was really pleased when he echoed my thoughts.

"I'm really looking forward to it. It's been a while since I've met someone as interesting as you," Marko said.

"Interesting, huh?" I laughed softly, my insides dancing in pleasure at the thought that he found me interesting.

"More than interesting. You're... refreshing. Definitely, someone I would like to get to know better," Marko said, his voice smooth. I bit my lip, trying to hold back the giggle bubbling up.

"Careful, Marko. Flattery like that could get you everywhere with me," I teased, keeping my tone playful. He chuckled softly.

"I'm sorry for what happened to you today, Melissa, but in a way I am also glad because if it hadn't happened, we might not have actually met," Marko said, making me smile.

"Funny how things work out, isn't it? I'm glad we met

too and I'm looking forward to breakfast," I replied, my heart fluttering with excitement.

"Great. Well, I will see you tomorrow. However, in the meantime, if you still can't sleep and need help to use up some of that pent up energy, let me know, I'm sure I can come up with some way to help you out," Marko teased, practically purring the words. It was all I could do to stop myself from begging him to come over and help me do just that.

Too soon, Melissa. Down Girl! I warned myself. It had been a while since I had been with anyone, and I certainly had an itch to scratch, but I had a feeling that what was starting between Marko and I, was way more than just sex. Marko was delicious, and he set my insides alight like no other. I wanted to take my time and explore that and see where this relationship could go.

"I might take you up on that someday, Marko. Goodnight," I replied with a chuckle.

"I hope you do. In the meantime, goodnight and sweet dreams, Melissa," he said in a voice dripping with sexiness as he hung up.

I hoped I did too.

The very thought sent a shiver of pleasure down my spine, and I grinned, biting my bottom lip to capture the giggle that threatened. I was so looking forward to spending more time with the man. Today might not have been great, but meeting Marko was definitely the highlight.

Suddenly, I had a lightbulb moment. Of course! Why

hadn't I thought of it sooner? Not only was the guy hot, but he was also an IT expert, which was exactly what I needed. I would just need to convince him to help me. Smirking, I thought of how much we'd flirted and our mutual attraction, and figured that might not be too difficult, not if I played my cards right.

I felt more optimistic knowing that I would see Mr Sexy Nerd in the morning and have someone to discuss the job with. How I would broach the subject, I wasn't sure, but I resolved to figure it out tomorrow. With a sigh of relief, I gathered up my duvet and crawled back into bed.

CHAPTER 8
MARKO

EARLY HOURS SATURDAY MORNING –
ANOTHER ENEMY REVEALED

When Melissa ended the call, it was nearly time for my next shift, and my face was sore from all the grinning and flirting. But my discomfort wasn't limited to my facial muscles—I also had a throbbing erection that demanded relief, so I took a quick shower to ease the tension.

Earlier, after I had escorted Melissa home following the robbery, I returned to my apartment for a few hours of much-needed sleep. Afterwards, feeling more refreshed, I reviewed the security footage Josh had obtained from the area around where the robbery took place.

Luckily, I was able to trace the journey of the motorbike all the way to an SUV, where they handed over Melissa's bag to someone inside before riding off again. I messaged Josh to run the plates and continue tracking where the guys on the bike went.

So, as I dried off, his response came through. He'd

identified the SUV owner. I stared at the name on the screen, stunned. Timothy Evans-Hughes was an MP and part of the Government. Why would he send men to grab Melissa's bag? How the hell was an MP involved with her? Shocked, I forwarded all the information to Miki for further investigation.

After dressing, I grabbed a quick bite to eat, filled a coffee flask for the long night ahead, and headed back to Melissa's place to begin my night shift.

During the short drive, I replayed our earlier conversations in my mind. Melissa had shown eagerness to see me again, which matched my own feelings. Her straightforwardness about her recent return to London and lack of a social life resonated with me—I didn't have much of a social life myself these days, not after spending the last year in particular bogged down with work to keep my family safe. I admired her honesty and directness.

Melissa's openness also hinted at a willingness to cooperate, which could prove beneficial for uncovering more about her connection to Mathieson and the MP. Despite the mystery surrounding her, I no longer viewed her as a threat to my family. In fact, I felt a protective instinct toward her, surprising myself with the intensity of my concern for someone I barely knew. However, virtual stranger or not, the woman was alone and in danger, and I wasn't about to let anything happen to her.

Somehow I sensed that Melissa Martin was poised to become a significant presence in my life, though I couldn't quite explain why I felt so strongly about it. It wasn't just physical attraction, there was something deeper that drew me to her. The anticipation of our upcoming breakfast date only heightened my eagerness to see her again, and I couldn't help the grin on my face as I joined Luca in the van, prompting a curious glance from my colleague.

"What's got that shit-eating grin on your face?" he asked.

I smirked and shook my head, not quite ready to divulge my growing feelings for Little Miss Pouty Lips. Thankfully, Luca didn't press further.

Once Luca left, I pulled out my flask of coffee and settled down for another night of surveillance. A few hours later, Miki called.

"The two guys on the bike were just hired help," he explained. "They were tasked with following Melissa and grabbing her bag when she left the bank. They handed it over to one of the MP's bodyguards. They were just two lowlifes, so I had them run out of town and warned to never come back to London again. I'm having the bodyguard picked up, too."

As I monitored Melissa's building, I opened my laptop and started digging into the MP's background. Initially, nothing significant popped up. Then, it dawned on me — Mathieson's real surname was Hughes, and his father was Ewan Hughes. The MP's name was Timothy Evans-Hughes; double-barrelled surnames often combined the mother's and father's surnames. Could Ewan Hughes and the MP be related?

After a bit of research, I found Timothy Evans-

Hughes's birth certificate, which confirmed his parents' names – Ewan Hughes and Elizabeth Evans. I located their marriage certificate and subsequent divorce papers. Bingo!

Simon Aiden Hughes, or Aiden Mathieson as he became known, and Timothy Evans-Hughes were half-brothers; the MP, being the result of his father's first marriage.

I called Miki, who sounded frustrated when he answered.

"What's up?" I asked.

"Someone hit the game last night!" he stated, blowing out a breath in frustration.

"The monthly?"

"Yeah. Everyone was shot at. Tereza got out, along with Vlad, but everyone else was taken out. I've had to shut things down for now."

"Fuck!"

"How many?"

"Five dead. Six were playing. Three businessmen from out of town, Jimmy the knife and Carson James and some Spanish guy that Carson brought along and vouched for. Turns out he went to the toilet mid-way through the game. We reckon he must have retrieved a gun from somewhere then came back and shot up the place," Miki said through clenched teeth.

"Geez. What about the shooter?"

"Escaped. A car pulled up shooting at the guys we had on security outside, just as the shooting started inside. It was well coordinated. They kept our guys pinned down until the Spanish guy was done inside. Then they drove off with him."

Fuck!

After the recent battles with the Malia Boys and Broxy's, Glowacki and my brother took over most of their operations so that our enemies couldn't. Things were split up between us and since we already had a casino and ran a high stakes annual poker game, we got a couple of their clubs and their underground gambling dens.

So, we were now running their high stakes monthly poker games too. These were illegal games, especially the high stakes games, so were by invitation only. To get in, you needed to be invited at the recommendation of a regular player. Carson Wells and Jimmy the knife were both regulars, so anyone they vouched for was considered fairly low risk. Obviously, that was a big mistake on our part.

Tereza was one of the croupiers who we used for these games. She was the head croupier at the small legitimate casino we ran and was Vlad's sister, so she was trustworthy. I was glad to hear Vlad had been there, he usually is when his sister is working but not always, so I was pleased he was able to get her out safely.

"Any idea who was behind it?" I asked.

"Nope, that's the problem. Our spies say that none of our usual enemies could have done it. They are all being closely monitored. Nobody knows where these guys have come from or who the Spanish guy is," Miki said, the frustration and confusion clear in his voice.

"I'm not sure if it could be related at all but I just found a link between Mathieson and the MP. Turns out Timothy Evans-Hughes is the son of Ewen Hughes from his first marriage to a woman called Elizabeth Evans and so he and Mathieson are half-brothers," I told him.

"Shit!"

He took a steadying breath.

"That seems a bit too much of a coincidence that we are attacked just at the time there is activity on the account and Mathieson's brother has the woman's bag grabbed, and you know Dad never believed in coincidences."

"Yeah, and Dad was usually right. Seems way too convenient not to be related. I'm still not sure what the link is to Melissa Martin though, but I'll find that out soon."

"I'll get the MP's bodyguard questioned, and I think it might be time to put some pressure on Nigel Simpson again. I think he knows a lot more than he is letting on," he told me before hanging up.

Hmmm. Suddenly having another enemy appear out of the woodwork when we had just discovered the link between the MP and Mathieson was too much of a coincidence, indeed. Maybe the half-brother was seeking revenge?

I emailed Josh to have him, and the rest of my guys, look into everything they could on the MP. He still had found nothing yet on Melissa. It was odd. There had to be some connection. Maybe I should just ask her outright. After all, if the MP had her bag grabbed, it meant he was after something he believed she possessed, and it suggested their relationship wasn't amicable. Perhaps he was the one working with Mathieson and, if so, my Little Miss Pouty Lips and I had a mutual enemy.

Leaning my head back against the headrest, I gazed at her window. It was dark, and the streetlight nearest the van was out, which was why we chose to park here. The one closest to the building was also out, meaning the back of the building was in complete darkness. But something caught my eye.

Was that movement?

Peering out of the window, I tried to make out something in the dark. After a while, I thought perhaps I was wrong and settled back in the chair. But I couldn't quite shake the feeling that something wasn't right. Ensuring the cab light was off, I quietly closed the van door and crept closer to the building.

CHAPTER 9
MELISSA
FRIDAY NIGHT – UP IN FLAMES

Something made me jolt awake. What was that? My heart raced as I lay listening intently.

At first, all I could hear was my breathing, but then a sound—a creak downstairs. Was it just the house settling or something more sinister? I held my breath, straining to hear. No, there it was again, a faint sound, like someone moving about downstairs. Shit, someone was definitely inside my home.

Moving quickly but quietly, I reached under the bed for my "to go" backpack. I slipped on the trainers kept beside the bed and grabbed a hoodie from the chair. Over my pyjamas, I threw on the hoodie and secured the backpack. Tiptoeing to the door, I cracked it open. A beam of light from a flashlight swept across the stairs, creeping upwards.

"Shit!" I muttered under my breath.

Rushing to the window, I opened it and tossed out a rope ladder my dad had rigged for emergencies. He'd always been prepared for the possibility of a getaway. Climbing down swiftly, I reached the ground just as a masked figure leaned out of my bedroom window. A knife whizzed past me, narrowly missing as I hit the ground hard. A heavy body landed on top of me, rolling us to the side.

Pushing against the weight on my chest, I tried to retaliate by aiming a headbutt at the masked intruder, but he moved just in time, my forehead glancing off his chin.

"Oooof!" he grunted.

"Melissa, it's me, Marko!" he whispered urgently in my ear, and I froze.

Marko? What was he doing here?

"What's going on?" he asked, getting up and tugging me with him further into the garden.

"Someone was in my house?" I said as he stopped under a tree and looked back towards my window.

Lifting his head, he sniffed the air.

"Shit, is that gas?"

Air whooshed out of my lungs as he pushed me hard up against the tree as the loud boom of an explosion assaulted my ears.

Debris flew through the air, and we ducked further under the branches, protected from the impact by the thick tree trunk and Marko's body pressed tightly against mine.

What the hell was that?

It took me a minute to process what had happened. The gas smell! That masked bastard had blown up my home.

We stayed cocooned behind the tree, our breathing

laboured as we tried to avoid the overpowering smell of gas and flames, waiting to ensure the explosion had ended before Marko cautiously peered around the trunk, scanning the surrounding area.

Pinned between him and the tree trunk, I couldn't move, so I simply watched him. The flickering flames cast shadows over his face, making it difficult to read his expression, but when he turned back to me his eyes sparkled with barely contained fury.

"What the hell happened?" he asked.

"I heard someone in my house," I began, keeping my voice low. "When I peeked out of my bedroom door, I saw a figure creeping up the stairs. I didn't want to stick around, so I got out through the window. That's when the person threw a knife at me."

"Shit, are you hurt?" Marko held me at arm's length, moving me around as he scanned my body for injuries.

"No, you appeared just in time and rolled me out of the way."

"Thank god," he said, hugging me to him again.

"What are you doing here?" I asked, narrowing my eyes at him, suspicion creeping through my bones. What was he doing here? How had he shown up just when someone was breaking into my home?

It seemed too coincidental that he had been there when I got mugged and was now here tonight when I was attacked in my home. I didn't believe in coincidences.

"We need to talk," we both said at the same time. Marko smirked.

"I'm glad we are on the same page about that, but I think it might be best to get you away from here in case the person responsible is still around," he said urgently, pulling me towards the garden gate.

Despite my suspicions about him, I didn't feel he was an immediate danger to me. In fact, I didn't feel he was a danger to me at all. It was inexplicable considering my current circumstances and the obvious fact that he kept turning up whenever something bad happened to me.

Yet ultimately, I doubted he was responsible for those bad things, but it was obvious something was going on with him. Just what it was and what it meant for me was what worried me. However, I needed to find out, and he was right, the man who attacked me could still be around. So, I let him lead me away.

Marko pulled out his mobile and made a call as he hurried me through the garden. Protesting seemed pointless; getting out of there right now seemed like a good idea. The heat from the flames was immense, and the crackle of the fire was loud in my ears. Sirens wailed in the distance, which I assumed were from fire engines racing towards us. I knew I would need to talk to the authorities about what happened, but getting away from the garden was definitely a priority.

As we reached the gate, I glanced back, and my heart sank. The gas explosion had left my home in ruins, flames tearing through the familiar walls. A profound sense of loss and despair overwhelmed me, leaving me numb with grief.

My beautiful home lay in shambles. It had once been a warehouse which my dad had lovingly converted into two apartments years ago. The larger flat on the second storey had been our home whenever we were in the UK. We used to rent the smaller flat below out. Thankfully, it was vacant at that moment, and with the closest neighbours over fifty feet away, separated by a driveway and garden, I took some solace in knowing that nobody had been hurt.

Tears threatened to spill as smoke stung my eyes and tightened my throat. Watching the flames engulf my home was overwhelming. Everything ramped up a notch; the roar of the flames grew deafening, the heat became suffocating, and sweat began to trickle down my neck, my breath coming in short, laboured gasps.

Then suddenly, the world around me seemed to blur. The cacophony of the fire was replaced by the harsh sound of my own panicked breathing. My vision swam, and I felt a wave of dizziness, as if the ground beneath me was shifting and I swayed unsteadily.

A firm hand gripped my arm.

"I've got you, sweetheart. It's just a panic attack. You're going to be fine," Marko said, his voice slicing through the panic. "Breathe, Melissa, take long, slow breaths," he urged gently, pulling me close.

Focusing on the calming words he mumbled into my hair, I tried to steady my racing heart, taking deep, measured breaths. Marko's presence grounded me as I fought to regain control. Finally, after several minutes of concentrating on my breath, the world stopped spinning, and I felt calmer again.

Glancing up at him, I felt a twinge of embarrassment. Having never experienced a panic attack before, the sensation was entirely new to me. With no history of anxiety, this was something I wasn't familiar with. The relief I felt for Marko's presence was immense, knowing he was there to guide me through the ordeal and I wasn't alone.

"Sorry about that," I said, hoping it hadn't put him off me.

"Don't be. You've been through a lot today. It's perfectly understandable," Marko assured me, kissing me on the forehead.

"Let's get you out of here," Marko said, wrapping his arm around my shoulders and leading me into the street and towards a white van nearby. It occurred to me that I had noticed it parked outside the house earlier today, but hadn't paid much attention to it at the time. I knew I should be questioning that revelation, but my brain just wasn't up to it right now.

Climbing inside, I glanced out of the window.

As I watched the fire licking the dark sky, I felt a bit dazed. If it hadn't been my home, I might have found it oddly beautiful. But seeing my house burn, taking with it all the memories of my parents, left me utterly distraught. It was all I had left of them, and now it was gone.

Tears began to fall uncontrollably, streaming down my face as I sat there, watching the fire crew battle the flames with their hoses. My mind was overwhelmed with memories. I remembered my mother passing away when I was only eight, leaving just Dad and me. Images of us playing in the garden together came flooding back.

I thought of the excitement of Christmas mornings, racing to their room to see if Santa had arrived. We always spent the holidays in London while Mum was alive, because she insisted that Christmas there was special. I wished I had managed to return for one last Christmas filled with memories here, instead of being alone in Monaco. If only I had known what was coming.

Marko leaned over and wrapped his arm around me once more, and I leaned into him. His presence felt comforting, and I desperately needed it. Resting my head against his chest, I let the sobs escape.

A few minutes later, the fire crew arrived.

"I don't want to leave you alone right now but someone needs to talk to them," Marko said. "I can deal with it if you don't feel up to it?"

"Please!" I sniffed and nodded my head gratefully as I rubbed at the tears with the back of my hand.

"I doubt that whoever did this will still be hanging around, but just in case, lock the door behind me and don't let anyone in but me. I'll have my eye on the van at all times. If you are worried about anything, blast the horn. Okay?"

I nodded again and Marko smiled.

"I'll be right back," he said, then kissed me gently on the forehead before heading off to meet them.

A warm glow enthused my whole being as I watched Marko walk away. I knew it was my responsibility, really, but after the shocks of the last couple of days, I just didn't feel like dealing with anything else right now. Having Marko here to help me was such a relief.

There was more to my Mr Sexy Nerd than simply the concerned bystander he appeared earlier, and we would definitely need to talk about exactly who he was and what he was doing in my life. However, for now, I was just glad he was here, and I didn't need to face all of this on my own.

As I peered out of the window, watching the fire crew attempt to douse the flames, tears threatened to engulf me once more. Brushing them away, I pulled a tissue from my bag and blew my nose loudly, refusing to give in to them, anger replacing my despair.

If Mathieson were still alive, I'd kill the bastard myself for dragging me into this mess and jeopardising my life. A searing rage bubbled up inside me, a blazing fire that scorched my insides just like the one that scorched my home. Fuck the bastard! And fuck the MP! If this was his work, I was going to make him pay. Whatever it took!

Just as that thought crossed my mind, a loud crash rang out, and yet another piece of my life shattered under the relentless pressure of the water being blasted towards the shell of what used to be my home. My anger turned to despair once more, and I could no longer keep hold of my emotions as the floodgates opened in earnest this time.

CHAPTER 10
MARKO
EARLY HOURS SATURDAY MORNING – A TASTE OF LITTLE MISS POUTY LIPS

"'ll be right back," I said, kissing Melissa on the forehead. I hated leaving her, but someone needed to talk to the fire crew, and she wasn't up to it. Besides, as I'd told her, I would be keeping close watch on the van and if there was any sign of danger, I would be by her side in seconds. I doubted the person responsible would be hanging around now however, not with the fire crew having arrived, however I wasn't going to take any chances. As long as I had her in my sights

After a quick chat with one guy where I confirmed nobody else was inside the building, I supplied them with our contact details then I left them to it and called Miki to appraise him of the situation.

"Fuck! You need to be careful. If this has anything to do with Mathieson, we need to find out, but we also need to avoid police scrutiny. You were a stranger to Miss Martin until a few hours ago and now you're a witness to

75

her being robbed and turn up at her house just when it blows up. We need to come up with an explanation for that if she or anyone else asks," Miki said, huffing in frustration.

"I know. Don't worry. I've got it covered. I'll just say that I was driving home after visiting Vlad at his flat, and passed her street because I wanted to know where to pick her up for breakfast in the morning. That will account for me being in the vicinity and I will come up with a plausible explanation for anything else if, and when, I need to," I replied, trying not to cringe when he shouted as I expected he would.

"What the fuck, Marko? What are you doing arranging to have breakfast with the woman?"

"We need to find out what her connection is to Mathieson and anything else she knows. Talking to her is the best way of doing that. Besides, we hit it off. There is something about her that draws me to her like nobody else. I don't believe she is any danger to us, and I really want to get to know her better," I said, keeping my voice firm.

Miki would not be happy with me messing around with Melissa when we didn't know her involvement in things, but after his involvement with Eilidh I figured he'd understand.

There was silence for a few seconds, and I knew Miki was mulling things over. I just hoped that he had faith in me and didn't order me back home and put someone else in my place watching over Melissa. Because pakhan or not, that was one thing I would not obey him on.

"Well, in that case I believe in your judgement on the matter, but something is going on here and obviously Miss Martin is in danger, so just watch your back," he replied, sighing heavily.

Raking my hand through my hair, I sighed myself, but it was one of relief.

"I'll get in touch with my contact in the Fire Brigade who investigates suspected cases of arson. He will ensure that the outcome of any investigation is simply a gas explosion with no foul play. I'll also let Vlad know about your alibi, just in case the police or the fire brigade follow up on it anyway," Miki said.

"Good. I will stay with Melissa and keep her safe," I told him.

"Fine. Keep me informed," he said before hanging up.

The fire would be officially labelled as an accident, and the earlier robbery would remain unsolved. That would ensure that whatever was going on here wasn't linked to my family through my involvement.

When I had Josh hack the security in the area around the site of the robbery, he had copied what I needed, then corrupted the images so that nothing significant could be seen. The police officers investigating it wouldn't be able to identify the culprits or link it to the MP.

With the crime report reference provided to Melissa for her insurance, that would be the end of it. All going well the two incidents wouldn't raise any real suspicion and would soon be forgotten about, at least for the law. It would be an entirely different story for Melissa of course.

I sighed, my thoughts drifting back to Little Miss Pouty Lips and the danger she was facing. It was crucial to uncover her connection to Mathieson and whatever else was happening in her life, but that could wait until tomorrow. Melissa had been through enough today. We would talk in the morning after she had rested.

It was a bit presumptuous to inform the head fireman that Melissa would stay with me and could be reached through my mobile, especially since I hadn't told her that yet. However, she had mentioned having no close friends in London, so the only alternative would have been a hotel, which wasn't an option. I wasn't about to let her out of my sight.

Little Miss Pouty Lips had been robbed, her home blown up, and someone had even tried to throw a knife at her. Her situation was far more precarious than I had realised, and my instinct to protect her was on high alert. From now on, her safety would be my main priority. My fists clenched as I walked to my van, where Melissa was safely settled. Anyone who threatened her would face my wrath.

Overwhelmed by a fierce protectiveness that I couldn't explain, not to mention a possessiveness I had no right to feel, I reminded myself she wasn't mine. Until a couple of days ago, I hadn't even known she existed, and until yesterday, we had never met. Yet, I couldn't help myself. I liked her. A lot.

My cock certainly agreed with me because it kept twitching at the mere thought of her and had done ever since I first saw her driving licence photograph. The bloody unruly thing had a mind of its own.

Even though I hadn't established if she was a threat to my family or not, my intuition told me Melissa wasn't and I couldn't wait to get to know her better.

As I climbed into the van, I discreetly adjusted myself. Now was hardly the time to be getting horny, I berated myself, glancing at Melissa. She was crying quietly, her whole body shaking in her effort to hold on to her emotions. My heart constricted tightly in my chest.

Wanting to comfort her, I leaned over and put my arm around her, tugging her onto my lap. Thankfully, her being so upset had brought my cock back under control and she snuggled close, turning her head towards me and burying it into my chest. Holding her tightly as she sobbed, I vowed then that whoever caused this was going to pay. If I got a hold of the guy responsible, I would kill him with my bare hands.

My hands stroked her back and her head and I kissed her forehead, wishing I could take away her pain. Outwardly I appeared calm, but inside my heart pounded and my mind was filled with anger. What the fuck was going on here? Who was trying to hurt my woman?

Shit! My woman? She wasn't mine, but by god, I wanted her to be and right now, with her curled up in my arms, it felt like she was. Things were moving fast between us, but I wasn't about to slow it down. I wanted Melissa Martin, and I was going to do whatever it took to make her mine.

My mouth twisted wryly as I thought about how I'd mocked Ash and Miki for falling for their women so quickly, and how even until yesterday I had been so sure I didn't need what they had and was not at all jealous. Obviously, I had been in denial, and I was turning out to be just as bad as them.

We sat there for a while, and I simply held my Little Miss Pouty Lips and let her cry. She needed to let it out.

When Melissa's sobs eventually died down, I moved her gently off my lap.

"I'm taking you to my apartment," I told her.

Melissa didn't protest, and in fact said nothing as we drove across the city. She simply lay her head back against the seat and gazed out of the window, probably trying to process everything.

When we got to the flat, I guided her to a spare bedroom and straight into the ensuite.

"Take a shower, sweetheart. You'll feel better after it. I will find you something to wear then you can take a nap," I told her before handing her some towels.

"Just call if you need me," I said.

She simply nodded, looking a bit dazed as I left her to it.

I grabbed a T-shirt and some gym shorts from the master suite where my brothers and I kept spare clothes for when we stayed here. Returning to the guest bedroom, I left them on the bed for her. Given our size difference, they were the best I could offer for now.

After quickly grabbing a shower myself, I put on some

fresh joggers and a T-shirt before heading to the kitchen. Melissa had quite a shock, so preparing some sweet tea and buttered toast seemed like a good idea. When she finished her shower, she padded through to the kitchen, and I handed them to her.

"I've put sugar in it to help with the shock," I said as she took a tentative sip.

"Thanks." She smiled with a sigh as she took a seat at the breakfast bar.

Melissa looked so cute in my oversized clothes, and I felt that possessive surge again. I let her sip her tea and watched as she nibbled absently on the toast.

"I know we need to talk, but it might be better to leave that until morning and get some sleep first," I told her when she was done.

She nodded, and I quickly tidied up.

"Let's get some rest," I said, turning towards the bedrooms, expecting her to follow, but she remained sitting and seemed to have zoned out. "Earth to Melissa," I said, smiling.

"Sorry," she replied, looking into my eyes.

"Let's get you to bed," I said, but neither of us moved. We just stared at each other, and my world shrunk to nothing but her.

I loved the colour of her eyes, such a beautiful green. They were stunning and I could easily get lost in them.

Melissa licked her lips, and my eyes were drawn to that luscious pouty mouth. Before I realised what I was doing, I took hold of her neck, pulled her head towards me and kissed her.

Oh god! Her lips were as soft as they looked and yielded easily to me. My tongue sought entrance, forcing them to part as I devoured her mouth and suddenly she was kissing me back with as much passion. Our tongues vied for domination as our hands roamed each other's bodies.

All I could think about was her. I was consumed by the need to touch her. Pushing her T-shirt up, I cupped her bare breasts, squeezing them gently. Her nipples hardened under my fingers and my left thumb circled her areola as I reached up with my right hand, cupping the back of her head while I kissed her deeply again. She moaned into my mouth, the sound making my dick jerk and my mouth smirk.

My hand moved from her breast down to the juncture of her thighs and slipped under the waistband of the gym shorts. I cupped her mound and groaned at the slickness there. She was wet for me, and I couldn't think of anything better than sinking my cock into her tight pussy.

The thought brought my movements to a halt, and I broke off the kiss. What the hell was I doing taking advantage of her when she was vulnerable? Melissa had been through a lot and wasn't thinking straight. I wanted her badly, but this wasn't the time.

When she reached for my face, I moved back a step, my palms facing toward her.

"We need to stop, you've been through a lot in just a

few short hours, and I don't want to take advantage of you," I said, my voice strained with the effort it took to get myself back under control.

"You're not," she said, reaching for me again, this time grabbing my hand.

"I want this, I want you, and I could definitely use the distraction from my thoughts right now. Please, Marko," she pleaded, and my conviction to be a gentleman waned.

"Are you sure?" I smiled, holding my breath for her reply. If she hesitated, I'd back off, but I couldn't help hoping she didn't.

"Hell yeah!" she said, grinning, and that was all it took. I pounced, kissing her like my life depended on it.

My Little Miss Pouty Lips tasted so good; I couldn't get enough of her. My hands roamed her body again. After quickly stripping her, I lifted her up onto the breakfast bar and pushed her down, so she lay naked before me. My eyes took in every inch of her from top to toe and back again, and I thought I might come in my pants. My heart was beating so loudly I was sure she must hear it.

"You're fucking gorgeous!" I told her, licking my lips in anticipation of tasting her.

Quickly, I removed my clothes, thankful for the condom in the pocket. These weren't my joggers; they were Luca's I believed. I wasn't sure, and right now, I didn't care. Whoever owned them, I was bloody grateful to them. I hadn't anticipated doing anything with Melissa, so I didn't have any protection of my own. It would certainly have broken the mood to go out to get some.

Fate must finally be smiling on me.

I tossed the joggers on the floor and ripped open the pack with my teeth before placing it on the worktop next to us.

Little Miss Pouty Lips checked me out, and from the look on her face, I thought she liked what she saw. Thank fuck! Because I bloody loved what I saw. I gulped and licked my lips again as I looked at her lying there, waiting for me.

Melissa squirmed as I settled between her legs and pulled her towards me. I took a nipple into my mouth, sucking hard. She clutched my shoulders as I pushed our bodies into the worktop, determined to get as close to her as possible. The feel of skin on skin threatened to make me lose it, but I took a deep breath as I reached between us and let my fingers explore right where my cock wanted to be.

My Little Miss Pouty Lips gasped and ground against me, and I built up the pressure, pinching and rubbing her clit while my tongue flicked, licked, and sucked on her nipple. She was so wet for me, and my cock was rock hard, making its desire to sink into her wet folds known. Not yet, patience! I told it as I kissed my way to her other nipple and tugged lightly on it, causing her to arch towards me.

While using my thumb to circle her tight little nub, I pushed one finger deep inside her, then another. I loved the tightness of her wet pussy stretched around my fingers, and I thrust them in and out faster and faster as she ground harder against me, riding them. The feel of her was amazing, and I couldn't wait to sink into her with my cock, but I needed her to come first, although it was getting harder to hold out.

"Oh god, Marko, I'm coming!" she shouted as her orgasm burst from her.

Melissa's eyes rolled back in her head, and I groaned at the look of ecstasy on her face. God, she was beautiful.

Seeing her like that made me feel like a goddamn sex god and she hadn't even had my cock yet. I smirked as I removed my fingers and lick them while she watched me trying to get her breathing under control.

"You taste amazing, Little Miss Pouty Lips." I smiled, then dipped down between her legs and took a long lick through her slit, repeating it several times, making her whimper and clutch at my head as her orgasm built again.

Jesus, she turned me on. I had to be inside her, but I was determined to make this last.

CHAPTER 11
MELISSA

Hot damn! Oh, my! Mr Sexy Nerd could really kiss. Not to mention the other things he could do with those enticing lips of his. That was the best orgasm I had ever had and the way my body was continuing to react to him, I knew it would not be a one off.

The minute he pressed his lips to me I was a goner. And it was just getting better and better. I felt like I couldn't get enough of him as he devoured me, our tongues vying for domination, our hands roaming each other's bodies.

My whole being buzzed with energy, and I felt more alive than I had in months. My body literally felt like it was burning under his touch, the chemistry between us was so potent.

I'd been going around in a bit of a daze since losing my dad. I hadn't been feeling much of anything lately.

After the initial grief wore off, and the crying stopped, I'd just felt numb. However, Marko made me feel again, and it was wonderful and I sure as hell didn't want it to stop.

My Mr Sexy Nerd's hands were back on my breasts, cupping and squeezing them. I believed Mr Sexy Nerd might be a boobs man.

"I love these," he murmured between kisses.

Yep! Definitely a breast man! I just barely stifled the girlish giggle bubbling inside. I couldn't help it. The way Marko kissed me as he played with my boobs made me feel almost giddy with pleasure.

Mr Sexy Nerd pulled back and looked at me, and the look in his eyes made the butterflies in my stomach go mad. We were both panting for breath and his half-closed eyes, dazed with lust were likely a mirror image of my own.

"You taste so good, Melissa, and you look so sexy lying there spread out ready for me," he said, his voice hoarse as his eyes roamed my body, his hands gently caressing my curves in a slow delicious torturous way.

I gulped; my mouth suddenly dry as I mimicked his action, taking in the sight of him in all his naked glory. The man was ripped. It took a lot of work to make a body look that good and I took my time appreciating it.

That is one sexy nerd!

My gaze roamed his body, returning repeatedly to his well-defined torso with its six pack that I wanted to lick so badly that my dry mouth watered. Yum!

My eyes flicked downward quickly, and I gulped

again. His cock was glorious, big, and hard. Bigger than the other men I'd had, but not so big I worried I couldn't take him. Of course, I'd only had a few relationships, so had little to go on, but I was pretty sure most guys wouldn't be unhappy to be packing what Marko was packing. And what he was packing right now was standing to attention. As I stared at it, the thing jerked as if trying to reach me. It looked almost painful.

Well, we can't have that!

Sitting up, I reached out and took it in my hand as he closed the distance between us again. My pussy ached with need as I clutched at his shoulders while he pushed me back against the worktop.

"I need you inside me, Marko," I practically begged him.

My pussy was throbbing with anticipation, and I squirmed as he settled between my legs, pulling me towards him, taking a nipple into his mouth, sucking hard.

"Not yet, sweetheart. Soon, but I want you to shatter again for me first," he murmured against my ear as his hand reached between us.

By the sounds of things, we were going to be here for a while I thought, thrilled at the prospect. I really wanted him inside me, but if he had plans to give me another earth-shattering orgasm first, well who was I to complain?

Doubt crept into my mind. I had never had multiple orgasms with anyone, what if it wasn't possible?

"What if I can't?" I asked.

"Oh, honey. Believe me, you will," he purred before taking my mouth.

As we kissed, his palm cupped my mound, and I cried out as my core clenched. My clit throbbed urgently, and I pushed my hips into his hand. Grinding against him until he took the hint.

My chest heaved and my breathing was erratic as Marko's fingers explored right where I wanted them. Unable to stop myself, I ground against him like a wanton thing, needing the friction to ease the pressure of my throbbing clit. Mr Sexy Nerd's fingers pinched and rubbed me while his tongue flicked, licked and sucked on my nipple and I could swear there was a direct line from my nipple to my clit as everything he did sent shivers down my body and drenched his fingers in my juices.

Marko kissed his way to my other nipple, tugging lightly on it as I arched my back towards him desperate to get closer to his mouth and that gifted tongue. He moved his fingers so that he could push one, then another, inside me while using his thumb to circle my nub. I loved the stretch of his fingers inside me, filling me as he thrust them in and out, making me grind harder against him, riding his fingers faster and faster.

"Yes, Marko," I shouted as another orgasm burst from me.

Panting hard, I slowly came down from my orgasmic high and watched in shock as he dragged his fingers out of me and licked them, smirking. No other guy had ever done that before. I felt like I should be embarrassed about it, but the way he seemed to enjoy my taste was strangely pleasing.

"I really love how you taste when you come for me, Melissa," he said and before I knew what he was doing, his mouth was on my pussy and he took a long lick through my slit.

Holy fuck! He wasn't trying for another one. Was he?

As he repeated the action several times, dragging his tongue slowly through my slit before sinking his tongue into my hole, I realised he was indeed. Surely that wasn't possible?

But it seemed Marko was determined to prove it was. I whimpered and moaned, clutching at his head, shocked that I could actually feel another orgasm building again. My god this man really knew how to turn me on.

My moans became louder as he thrust that talented tongue of his inside me several times, while his hands reached for my breasts again, teasing my nipples, slowly plucking them, then rubbing them until I squirmed under his torturous assault on my senses.

My body tingled with desire, but I needed more.

"Please, Marko, I need you now," I begged, pulling him up my body.

He smirked as he lined himself up and kissed me hard.

"Fuck!" I cried into his mouth, tensing with the shock as he breached me in one swift thrust.

My Mr Sexy Nerd felt so bloody big, but I clutched him to me, holding him in place as I panted out breaths and forced my body to relax.

After several seconds, my pussy adjusted to the intrusion and he slowly and deliberately started to thrust, pulling himself almost all the way out before plunging back right to the hilt each time. Marko pounded into me over and over, keeping his body close to me and kissing me deeply all the time, and I loved the full body contact as he took me. Wrapping my legs around him, I held him even closer.

Marko sped up frantically and his rhythm became erratic as he came close to release and my own built yet again.

"Yes!" he cried as I screamed his name, our release exploding in tandem.

Geez, I had never been a screamer. In fact, I had always made myself quiet until now, too embarrassed to truly let go. Yet with Marko, I not only let myself go completely, but I also bloody well shattered for him, just like he said I would.

Dear god, the man was bloody good. I smirked as he continued to thrust, ensuring we rode out every bit of our orgasm.

My inner voice did a little dance and chanted, *"I just had amazing sex!"*

And that's when I came back down to earth. Oh shit!

Marko pulled away from me and I froze unable to move, my eyes squeezed tightly shut. What the hell was I thinking? We'd had sex without protection!

My eyes flew open at the sound of rubber snapping and

I was just in time to see him pull a condom off and throw it in the rubbish bin nearby.

Oh, thank fuck! How the hell did he get that on without me realising? Mr Sexy Nerd's got skills! Those thoughts all bombarded my mind at once as relief poured through me. The man might have given me the best sex of my life, but Marko was still a stranger, and I didn't want to risk pregnancy.

My mum had been a single mother until she met my dad, and while she never complained about that, I knew the early years had been hard for her and so I always swore that wouldn't happen to me. When I had kids, I would be in a solid, loving relationship, and they would be planned.

Marko returned to me and pulled me into his arms, kissing me on the tip of my nose, oblivious to where my mind had been.

"That was bloody amazing!" he said with a shit-eating grin that made me want to swoon.

As I watched him turn and open a drawer, I noticed a tattoo on his left shoulder, but I didn't get any time to inspect it as my eyes dropped to his tight ass. Oh my god, it was so biteable!

Marko noticed me staring, and that grin was back in seconds. My cheeks flamed at being caught ogling him. Though why it should bother me after what we had just done was anyone's guess.

Reaching his hand out, Marko ran his fingers gently down the side of my face, and my body shivered in pleasure at his simple touch.

Hell, I was in deep. How had the guy got under my skin so quickly?

Using the cloth he took from the drawer, he wiped me, cleaning my lady parts. Squirming, I fought the urge to close my legs as his hand moved between them. The intimate gesture overwhelmed me, making my cheeks grow hotter and I couldn't look him in the eye. I didn't understand my reaction since we'd already been far more intimate that this should not bother me at all.

"Are you okay, sweetheart?" he asked, his eyes searching mine.

My voice failed me and so I simply nodded.

Marko looked at me and raised his eyebrows, but thankfully said nothing and simply reached down and handed me my clothes. I hurriedly dressed, still not quite able to look at him. My cheeks felt hot, and I knew I was acting weird, but my mind was a mess.

Maybe Marko had been right, and we shouldn't have continued earlier. It seemed I hadn't been thinking straight when I pleaded with him to continue because now that I was over the shock of everything that had happened, I was beginning to wonder about things. In fact, my mind was whirling with unanswered questions. Mainly about Marko.

As I'd thought before, it couldn't be a coincidence that he appeared right after I was robbed, or again right after someone broke into my home. So, who was he and what did he want from me? Could he be working for the MP? Or be a police officer investigating me? If anything, it was more likely to be the former rather than the latter, and yet I didn't feel any danger when I was in his company. But was there?

Worrying at my bottom lip, I finally looked into his eyes and my breath hitched at the open expression of longing I saw there.

No, I didn't think a man who looked at me like that was a danger to me. Well, not physically anyway. My heart however, that was another matter.

As if reading my thoughts, Marko pulled me close and kissed the top of my head.

"You're safe here with me, honey," he murmured against my hair. "Let's take a nap, then we can talk," he said, putting his arm around my waist and leading me through the hall.

I had expected him to take me back to the guest room, but instead, he led me into his own. My heart pounded as he pulled back the covers, and though I knew I should have protested, I stayed silent. The thought of being alone right now felt unbearable. He gently instructed me to get in, closing the curtains before slipping into bed beside me.

Fatigue washed over me, a heavy, undeniable wave. Marko pulled me close, and I nestled into his embrace, the warmth of his body providing a comfort I needed. A deep sigh escaped my lips as my eyes fluttered shut. Whatever the future held, I would face it later. For now, I burrowed deeper into his arms and allowed sleep to take over.

CHAPTER 12
MARKO
SATURDAY AFTERNOON – TIME TO TALK

My senses were filled with warmth and a delicious scent as I slowly came awake. It felt good waking up with Melissa snuggled close to me. Having her beside me brought me a peacefulness I hadn't felt since I was a child. I sighed in contentedness, but didn't open my eyes, not wanting that blissful moment to end yet.

Little Miss Pouty Lips was draped across my chest, one leg over mine, and it struck me how well she fit next to me. Breathing deeply and taking in Melissa's citrusy scent made my cock awaken. She shifted slightly and I could feel her watching me. I let my eyelids flicker open, a slow smirk spreading across my face when I saw her staring back at me.

"If you keep staring at me like that, I'm going to have to do something about it, and while I would love to keep you in bed with me for the rest of the day, we have things to talk about, and you also need to deal with what has happened to your home," I told her in amusement, although I was kind of hoping she kept staring so I could make good on my threat.

Down, boy! I told my cock as he jumped in agreement with my thoughts.

Melissa cleared her throat and with a small smile, pulled out of my embrace, and I couldn't help the sudden feeling of loss now that she was no longer in my arms.

"You're right, we need to talk. Then I need to contact my insurance company and deal with everything," she said.

Melissa's teeth sank into her lip as silence enveloped her, her thoughts visibly swirling behind her eyes; a vulnerability settled over her features. Reaching out, I pulled her close, hugging her tightly. I understood. The weight of her recent losses, of first her father and now her home, was palpable.

"Hey, I'm sorry about what happened. I know this must be very difficult for you, but I am here and happy to help so you don't have to feel alone or overwhelmed," I told her, wanting her to know that I meant what I said.

"Thanks," she said, her smiling reaching her eyes this time, before giving me a quick peck on the cheek then climbing out of bed.

"Can I grab another shower?" she asked.

"Sure, sweetheart. You use the one in here, and I'll take one in the other room. But wait a minute, and I'll get you something else to wear," I told her.

Melissa had gone to bed in the clothes I had given her earlier, but I always slept in the buff. Her eyes widened and her cheeks flamed at the sight of my naked body walking towards her. I bit back a smile. Considering what we had done earlier in the kitchen, I hadn't expected her to be so shy, and I found it endearing.

After opening the wardrobe, I deliberately lingered there for a few seconds longer than necessary, hoping she was checking out my bum.

A smirk tugged at my lips for being so vain. Normally, I wasn't, even though I worked hard to stay in shape. My whole family did; we needed to be ready to fight for our lives, making fitness a necessity rather than vanity.

However, I found that I really wanted Melissa to like my physique. Her opinion of me mattered more than anything at that moment, more than I cared to admit, actually. I wanted her to feel the same attraction for me I felt for her. That was the most important thing to me right then.

"You can wear the shorts again and this T-shirt until we sort out some proper clothes for you," I told her, handing her the T-shirt. My smirk increased when I saw that she had indeed been checking me out and from the look on her face, she liked what she saw. I mentally high-fived myself.

Wither her face aflame, Melissa quickly grabbed the T-shirt, mumbled, "thanks," and turned to leave. Before she could, I grabbed her and planted a quick, chaste kiss on her mouth. I wanted to do so much more than that, but if I did, I wouldn't get any answers today, and unfortunately, with her life in obvious danger, I needed to.

So rather than pushing her down on the bed and taking her the way I wanted to, I took a cold shower instead. It did nothing for my libido because all I could think of was her—how she tasted when I kissed her, how she responded to my touch, her moans of pleasure as I fingered her and how she felt surrounding my cock with her tight wet pussy.

My thoughts tortured me as the freezing water battered off my hard-on, adding to the painful pressure instead of relieving it. Sighing heavily and wishing I had given in to my needs and taken my Little Miss Pouty Lips back to bed, I instead took the source of my discomfort in hand and quickly relieved myself, knowing I wouldn't be able to function properly otherwise.

Eventually, after I had got myself back under control, I dried off and headed into the kitchen where I could hear Melissa moving about.

Little Miss Pouty Lips was boiling the kettle when I arrived, so I took over and made some coffee and sandwiches while she contacted her insurance company. Afterwards, we sat down to eat. I watched her intently as she nibbled on her lunch, lost in thought.

Melissa really was beautiful. The moment I saw this woman's photo, I'd liked her, but that was physical, of course. Now that I had spent time with her, I was even more enamoured. I just hoped my intuition about her was not wrong. If she turned out to be an enemy to my family after all, I was not sure how I was going to cope. Well, I guessed it was time to find out. I was just about to open my mouth and tell her it was time to talk when she spoke.

"Marko, I like you. I really do, but I have some questions I need answered before I can open up to you any more than I have already," she said.

"I will answer whatever I can," I told her with a smile.

My insides did a happy dance while I fought to keep my outer-self calm. She liked me. I wanted to pick her up and swing her around, then lay her down and ravish the hell out of her. But I reminded myself yet again that now was not the time.

I really couldn't help feeling elated, though. Earlier, when she had acted standoffish after we'd had the best sex of my life, I had been devastated. I'd tried not to take it personally because she'd been through so much and I figured that she was simply tired and feeling the effects of the day she'd had. But deep down, I had worried she'd regretted what we'd done. Her words now had bolstered my ego and relief filled me.

"What were you doing at my house last night just when someone was breaking in?" she asked.

"Straight to the point. Good," I replied, glad. The quicker we got things out in the open, the better. I wasn't exactly sure what to tell her, but quickly decided the full truth was best if I wanted us to have any kind of relationship, and I most definitely did.

So, I told her, and she simply listened.

Well, I told her everything except that Mathieson was

not just missing but had been killed by us. I hoped Miki wouldn't be annoyed with me revealing so much so soon, and I sure as hell hoped I was making the right call, but it felt like the best thing to do.

Melissa's eyes widened at certain points, and she looked genuinely upset when I mentioned Krissa. Despite her visible distress, she remained silent, which I was grateful for. Her quietness made it easier for me to stay calm and matter-of-fact. If she had bombarded me with questions or offered too much sympathy, I might have lost my composure. The thought of how Krissa had died still ignited a deep anger in me, and I didn't want to scare Melissa off. It was already going to be challenging enough for her to accept me being Bratva, so I didn't want her to see me angry. If she did, she might be even more frightened, and that would jeopardise my plans to keep her close.

When I finished speaking, she still just stared at me. I let her take her time, waiting for her to process everything I'd shared, all the while praying she wouldn't want to run from me once she had.

CHAPTER 13
MELISSA
SATURDAY AFTERNOON – ALLYING WITH THE BRATVA

When I'd asked Marko what he was doing at my house, I had watched as he pursed his lips, narrowing his eyes while he obviously decided how best to answer. I'd wondered at that moment if he would tell me the truth or make up some story, but then he started talking.

As I sat quietly listening, I couldn't hide my reaction, especially when he talked about what had happened to his sister, Krissa. That was so awful.

After he had told me what I assumed was everything he planned to, I just looked at him in stunned silence, trying to process it all. Was this for real?

I felt like I had woken up two days ago and walked into my very own crime novel, and I seemed to be one of the main protagonists. I shouldn't have been so shocked considering I hadn't led the most law-abiding life myself;

however, "What the hell?" and "Oh shit!" were really all I could think in response to what I'd just been told.

Pulling air into my lungs, I took a deep, steadying breath as I desperately tried to get my thoughts in order.

"Okay, let me get this right. You're from a Russian Bratva family, and your brother is the pakhan?" I said, trying to make sense of everything.

He nodded.

"A corrupt lawyer called Aiden Mathieson blamed your family for his father's imprisonment and subsequent suicide and his family's struggles afterwards."

Another nod.

I didn't mention that the same bloody lawyer was none other than my biological father. Not yet, I was keeping that little nugget for later.

"And he was secretly using your enemies to attack you in various ways over the last few years as some sort of retaliation?"

Marko still said nothing, just making sounds of agreement as I continued to relay my understanding.

"And although you managed to thwart his attempts to take your family down, you are not sure that he was working alone, so you traced one of his bank accounts and it led you to me and you want to know what I have to do with him?"

"That's about right," he said.

Woah! Geez, I knew my biological father said he was an evil man, but I didn't think it meant he'd been trying to take down a Russian mafia family, like his father before him, apparently.

"That's why you were around when I was robbed and when someone blew up my home? You've been following me?" I asked for final clarity.

My voice rose a bit at the end of this last question as my nerves started to take hold. Maybe I was in danger from him after all? Marko obviously sensed my worry as his voice took on a soothing quality when he next spoke.

"Yes, Melissa, but you are not in any danger from me. I promise. However, I need you to tell me how you are connected to Aiden Mathieson? It is very important that you are truthful because you are obviously in danger from someone. I will help you with that, but I can't do it if I don't know who is endangering you," he said, and I released the breath I didn't know I was holding as I relaxed a little at his statement.

It was a relief to hear that he wasn't a direct threat to me, though he was right—I was definitely in danger.

I chewed on my lip, deep in thought. He had promised to help me, and I knew I needed all the allies I could get. Besides, I had already realised that Marko's help was crucial. His tech skills were exactly what I required. I just hadn't figured out how to ask him for help, but it seemed like fate had provided a clear path forward. So, I bit the bullet and decided to be as truthful with him as he'd been with me.

"Aiden Mathieson is my biological father, but I only just discovered that," I rushed out. I saw his lightbulb moment when I told him my mother was called Jessica Adams.

"That's why there was an account in her name," he said, nodding.

"I guess so," I replied before telling him everything I knew about Mathieson and the MP.

Marko looked pissed when I told him how Mathieson had tasked me with obtaining the evidence to bring the MP to justice.

"Why the hell did he ask you to do that?" he asked incredulously.

"Well, I have some special skills that he seemed to think made me the ideal candidate unfortunately," I replied, my voice laced with irony.

Then, I told him about my dad being a cat burglar and me having the same skills. Not something I had ever wanted to disclose to anyone, but I needed his help to break into the MP's place and get the evidence Mathieson alluded to, so I'd had to suck it up and tell all.

His eyes widened in amazement when he heard, then he smirked sexily.

"I've always liked a woman with skills. You've got hidden depths, Melissa, and I'm looking forward to peeling back each of your layers and discovering all of your secrets," he grinned and I gulped hard, as my knickers got damp.

"Yes, please!" my inner voice screamed as I stared at him. He could peel back my layers anytime he wanted. And I didn't doubt for a second that I was the only one

with hidden depths. Marko had his own secrets, and I was eager to uncover them.

In fact, I wondered if we might start unearthing some of our secrets together right now. My mind raced with several intriguing possibilities, and I couldn't help but lick my lips. My cheeks flushed when I noticed the way he was grinning at me, clearly aware of the shift in my thoughts.

Suddenly feeling overheated, I blinked rapidly and turned away from that captivating grin and the mischievous sparkle in his eyes before my impulse took over and I jumped him. There would be time for that later, I hoped. For now, we still had important matters to discuss, so I pushed the tantalising thoughts aside and forced my focus back to the task at hand.

Fetching my backpack, I poured out the contents and showed him the letters. Once he'd read them, I opened my phone and pulled up the pictures I took of the photographs from the safety deposit box.

"These were what was stolen with my bag, along with a small dictaphone," I said before playing the recording of the phone conversation that had been on it.

Mr Sexy Nerd gazed at me with a mix of awe and admiration as I explained the precautions I had taken at the bank—how I'd split up the evidence, but made sure I had everything I needed on my person as well as in my bag. His smile, so undeniably sensual, made my cheeks flush and sent a tightening sensation through my core. The effect he had on me with just a look or a grin was electrifying. I was so screwed!

"There was another attack on one of our businesses yesterday, and I believe the MP might be behind it. It is likely we have a common enemy, Melissa. Even if it wasn't him, he sounds like a foul bastard anyway, so it looks like we need to work together and take him down," he said vehemently as I pondered his words.

"Besides, it gives me another reason to have you remain by my side." He winked, and his slow grin full of secret promise made me gulp.

My heart pounded, and I squirmed, looking away from him as I tried to push away the rush of sexual need I felt every time he looked at me like that.

Marko had laid out his family's moral code regarding women when he talked about his sister. I could respect that, but getting too entangled with this man and his family made me uneasy. Yes, I desperately needed an ally and had hoped to leverage Marko's IT skills, but could I really get in bed with the Bratva?

"You already did!" The annoying little voice in my head chimed in. My hand flew to my mouth as I stifled a cough to hide the giggle threatening to escape. The voice had a point—there was no denying it.

As I paced the floor, I chewed anxiously on my bottom lip. Danger was closing in, and I had already determined that I needed backup to stay safe. Marko was that backup. Yet, the idea of getting more personally involved with him made me hesitant. Engaging in criminal activities together was risky enough, but becoming emotionally entangled with him would complicate things even further.

My head was aching from all of this thinking. I'd returned to the UK for a quiet life. Why the hell couldn't danger have left me alone? It was as if I was a bloody magnet for it.

I'd sworn to leave the dangerous life behind and pursue something more stable. A brief brush with danger was one thing, as I had no choice if I was to navigate this current mess, but I refused to be pulled back into old habits and a world I'd only just escaped. The idea of getting involved with Marko felt like a slippery slope back to that world. Clearly, shutting down this growing attraction was the smartest move, no matter how good we were together.

However, as he quietly watched me, with his eyes full of admiration and his smile undeniably sensual, my body had other ideas. Damn it! Just his gaze made my knickers dampen, making a mockery of my resolve.

"Well, I'm a grown woman, I can resist his charms," I told myself. But despite my words, I wasn't convinced.

Huffing out a breath, I sunk heavily onto the sofa.

Maybe I should just grab the first flight out of here and never look back. But as soon as the thought crossed my mind, I knew it was unrealistic. No, I had to stay and face this head-on.

Mathieson had warned me that the MP would come after me—even before I knew anything concrete about him —and he had been right. Considering the events of the past twenty-four hours, it was clear the MP viewed me as a threat, a loose end that needed to be tied up. There was no escaping this mess.

More importantly, I was determined to bring that bastard down. He was a malevolent force who had torched my home and destroyed an irreplaceable part of my past. He needed to pay for what he'd done, and Marko was essential to achieving that. I resolved to work with him and keep things strictly business. It would only be a few weeks, maybe months at most. Surely, it wouldn't be too hard to keep my emotions in check and maintain my distance?

"Agreed!" I finally said, nodding.

"But first, I need to sort out some clothes and other necessities and then a place to stay," I told him.

Marko noticeably balked at the idea, and his smirk slipped. His eyes narrowed as he gazed at me.

"Melissa, you can use the spare room here if it makes you more comfortable but getting a hotel room is not only dangerous, as we don't know what the MP will do next, but also impractical. We will need to work together closely to obtain the evidence we require. It will be easier to do that if we are here together where I can protect you," he said, rising to loom over me.

"But…"

"You will stay here!" His voice was commanding, leaving no room for argument.

I shot him a glare, ready to protest, but then thought better of it and clamped my mouth shut. Biting back the retort I wanted to hurl at him, I took a deep, calming breath. His intense gaze locked onto me, waiting for a response.

Damn, the man was annoying. But I had to admit he was right, though. Staying here would make our collaboration smoother and keep me safer. And if I was honest, the idea of being alone in a hotel right now was frightening. Yet, it wouldn't help me maintain the distance I needed from him, and I could already feel my resolve starting to waver.

"Fine, but I still need clothes," I huffed, frustration evident in my tone.

Marko's smirk only fuelled my irritation. That smug look of his made me want to slap him. I realised I had capitulated far too easily. I should have fought harder, made him work for my agreement. Yet, despite my irritation, I couldn't tear my gaze away from those irresistibly curved lips of his.

Even though my mind protested, a thrilling rush surged through me at the thought of staying here with him. Marko's gorgeous smile, those well-defined abs, and the nerdy charm he exuded when wearing his glasses—who knew that was my type? I momentarily lost myself in admiration, only snapping back to reality when he pulled me into his embrace.

"Better stop looking at me like that if you want to hit the shops for some clothes before they close," he teased, planting a quick kiss on my lips.

My body betrayed me, swaying towards Marko on its own accord, seeking more, but he stepped back, turned me around, and gave me a playful swat on the bum, directing me toward the bedroom.

"Go get ready," he ordered with a chuckle that made my core ache with need.

So much for keeping things strictly professional, my resolve had lasted less than five minutes and the way my body responded to Marko showed me just how ridiculous that thought had been.

As I headed to the bedroom, with a wry smile, I admitted that it was useless to even try. Getting further involved with Marko might definitely be dangerous for my newly gained quiet life, but there wasn't any way to avoid it. I was already in way too deep. Resistance was futile.

Besides, we were about to embark on a perilous mission to bring a psychotic MP down. Who knew what would happen? We could end up dead. I shivered at the thought, but it was true. So why not just go with the flow and enjoy what moments I could? Just because we worked together and had a fling didn't mean I couldn't go back to my quiet life in the future.

By the time I grabbed my shoes and bag and returned to the livingroom, I had decided that was exactly what I would do. And, in the process, I intended on making some really great memories.

CHAPTER 14
MARKO

SATURDAY EVENING – ANOTHER ATTACK
ON MELISSA'S LIFE

While Melissa got ready to go out, I called Miki and gave him a quick update on everything I had found out.

He agreed that the MP sounded like a crazy guy and was definitely the most likely person behind the attack on our poker game. He was also happy that we may have the means of putting an end to him.

"Bring her in," he said.

"No, not yet. She's staying here with me. I'll bring her over to see you tomorrow," I replied, my voice firm.

Miki was quiet for a minute. I wasn't sure what he was thinking. As pakhan, he was rarely disobeyed, and I had never disobeyed him before, but I wasn't prepared to share Melissa yet. I wanted her to myself. That might have been selfish, but I didn't care. Whatever was between us was strong, and I wanted a chance to spend more time with her on my own.

I could hear Miki take a deep breath, and I braced myself for his annoyance. But to my surprise, he laughed instead.

"Marko, it sounds like you have staked a claim on this woman. You are as bad as the rest of us. Does she know yet?" he asked, sniggering.

"Erm, eh, no," I stuttered out, my equilibrium knocked for six when he continued to chuckle.

That wasn't at all the reaction I was expecting. Not in the least. I shook my head, regaining my composure.

"She's receptive to me, but no, she doesn't know yet that I have serious feelings about her," I told him in all honesty.

"Well, I'm sure you will enlighten her soon enough," he said, his amusement still obvious in his voice as he continued.

"Since she is likely going to be yours, I guess she needed to know who we are and what that means. Besides, from what you've told me, we need her help as much as she needs ours. We'll talk about everything when you get here tomorrow," he said, then hung up.

Well, that was easier than I had anticipated.

Next I called Trigger, gave him a quick update of the situation, and let him know we were heading out and to come over.

Trigger was one of our soldiers, a good friend, and completely loyal. I trusted him totally. He would drive us around today and provide additional security while we were out. This apartment was considered a safe house for us; few people knew of its existence, and it had an excellent security system. We rarely required additional security here, but as we were heading out, I didn't want to take any chances.

Somehow, the MP knew about Melissa. He knew she would go to the bank, and where she lived, and had obviously sent people after her. Although the initial attack against her was simply a robbery, the second attack was much more sinister. I doubted he'd be able to find her again now that she was with me, but I couldn't be sure of that. It was best to have backup just in case.

A short while later, I took Melissa's hand as we weaved through the bustling Covent Garden shopping centre.

"What do you think about this place?" I asked, glancing around at the array of shops. There were plenty of great places to shop in London, including the world famous Harrods, but I'd always liked this place. It had been a favourite of my mum and so I had fond memories of coming here with her as a child.

"Oh, I love it here," she said, her eyes lighting up as she spotted a familiar brand.

Dragging me towards the shop, she pulled me inside and I couldn't help but chuckle at her enthusiasm.

We spent a couple of hours browsing through racks of clothes in one shop after another. Melissa trying on various outfits, while I offered my opinion.

"That colour suits you," I commented as she emerged from the changing room in a vibrant dress.

She smiled appreciatively. "You think so?" Melissa twirled, the dress swishing around her legs.

"Yeah, definitely," I nodded, impressed by how well it complemented her.

When she was finished, we headed to the counter, and I started to hand my card to the cashier.

"Wait. I'm paying for this," Melissa insisted, pulling out her card and handing it over instead.

I was about to protest, as a deep-rooted need to protect and care for my woman warred with the need to respect her independence, but her determined look made me clamp my mouth shut. Melissa was mine, but she wasn't ready to admit that yet, so I wouldn't push her and risk our budding relationship just to assuage my need to provide. Besides, she was rich in her own right, so there was really no justification for me paying. Yet. One day, things might be different, but not today.

"Alright," I conceded with a smile. "But let me treat you to dinner at least."

"Deal," she said with a grin.

A little later, we settled into a cosy corner of a nearby restaurant, the soft glow of candlelight casting a warm ambiance.

"Cheers," I said, raising my glass of wine in a toast.

Melissa clinked her glass against mine.

"Cheers to surviving another day," she quipped, her eyes sparkling with amusement.

We enjoyed a leisurely meal, sharing stories and laughter as we delved deeper into each other's lives.

"So, tell me more about your family," Melissa prompted, leaning forward with genuine interest.

I recounted tales of growing up with my siblings, anecdotes about my father's strict yet caring nature, and a little about Miki's role as our Pakhan. Melissa listened intently, nodding along and occasionally interjecting with her own experiences.

As the evening progressed, my phone vibrated with a message from Miki. Melissa excused herself to freshen up, leaving me to read the text in peace.

Aw, shit! Another of our businesses had been hit. This time, it was one of our legitimate ones. Fuck!

"Bring Melissa in now!" Miki said at the end of the message.

Frowning at the phone, I shook my head. Nope, not happening.

"Tomorrow!" I texted back and turned down the volume, ignoring the vibration alerting me to his answer.

Miki wouldn't like me ignoring him, but tough. He would not spoil the evening I had planned. I would take the tongue lashing tomorrow if necessary. Tonight, I was going to be doing one of my own, which would be much more pleasurable. My cock jumped at the idea. And on that note, it was time to leave.

"Everything okay?" Melissa asked as she returned to the table.

"Another of our businesses was hit, so we need to

speak with my family and start making plans, but it will wait until tomorrow," I told her.

"Was anyone hurt?" she asked.

"No, but my brother is livid. However, we'll deal with everything tomorrow. For now, I have more enjoyable things in mind," I told her, grabbing her hand and kissing it.

I wanted Melissa to myself to get to know her better, just the two of us. Tomorrow was soon enough to explore ideas for the MP's downfall. This evening, I planned on exploring Melissa and her delightful body again, and nobody was going to spoil that, not even my brother, the Pakhan.

"Sounds good," she responded with a sultry smile that made me want to take her right there and then.

As we waited outside for Trigger to pick us up, I pushed her into the shelter of a nearby doorway and pulled her close, kissing her deeply the way I had wanted to all night. I groaned as she moaned into my mouth, losing myself in her. Our mouths battled for dominance, our tongues duelling as if they couldn't get enough of each other's taste. My hardness pressed against her stomach, and reluctantly, I pulled apart, willing my erection to behave long enough for us to get back to the apartment.

"If I don't put some distance between us, I'm afraid I might lose control and take you right here against the wall," I said, my voice low and thick, with a slight trace of a Russian accent noticeable from my lust.

Melissa's eyes widened, and a mischievous smile played on her lips.

"Maybe that wouldn't be such a bad thing," she teased, her hands tracing lightly over my chest.

My heart pounded at her touch, the heat of her fingers penetrating my shirt and sending shivers of excitement coursing through me. God, the woman drove me wild with need. I chuckled softly, and with effort, I forced myself to hold her at arm's length.

"As much as I'd love that, my brother would kill me if we were caught committing a sexual act in public. And I'm not sure you would enjoy that either," I said with a laugh.

She pouted playfully, making me grin wickedly. Pulling her to me again, I nipped at her earlobe and she squirmed against me once more.

"Are you an exhibitionist, my little cat burglar? Should I throw caution to the wind and take you right here where anyone could see? Is that what you want, sweetheart?" I whispered teasingly, grinding myself against her.

"No!" Her eyes widened, and she pushed at my chest, looking a little panicked.

"You are right, because while I have occasionally fantasised about having sex outside, a London street where others could see isn't quite what I'd had in mind. And I doubt I could get over the embarrassment of being caught," she said, her face flaming at the idea as she tried to step out of my embrace again. I loosened my hold on her but didn't let her go.

"Relax honey, we can keep the public displays of affection to kissing." I reassured her, chuckling and nuzzling at her neck.

"However, I am going to want to know more about those outdoor sex fantasies of yours later, and if you are into being taken against a wall, I'm sure I can arrange for a better venue for that, too," I said with a wink.

The wicked glint in her eyes told me she liked that idea, and I made a mental note to ensure that I fulfilled those particular fantasies later, as I took her hand once more and turned to head towards where Trigger was now parked waiting for us.

"I'll hold you to that," she replied, grinning up at me sexily.

Before I could respond, she pulled me to a stop again and tugged my head down to hers for another kiss. We were so lost in each other that neither of us heard the car approaching fast from behind.

"Marko!" Trigger shouted, alerting me to the danger.

"Down!" I screamed at Melissa as I threw us out of the path of the oncoming vehicle. It mounted the pavement and charged past us at full speed. We had been just a step away from the large doorway, and throwing ourselves inside saved us from being crushed under the wheels.

Pulling Melissa tight to me, I looked her over. "Are you okay?"

She nodded, her eyes wide with fear. That was close, too fucking close.

Grabbing her hand, I tugged her across the road.

"Fucking bastards!" Trigger shouted, shooting at the vehicle. The back window shattered, but the car continued to barrel away from us.

"Let's get out of here," I told him. He jumped into the driver's side, and we got in the back. He spun the car around, and we revved off away from the scene and any unwanted police attention.

CHAPTER 15
MELISSA

LATE SATURDAY EVENING – GOING TO THE ESTATE

arko bundled me into the back of the car and pulled me close. I clung to him, shaking. Heck, that had been close.

"I can't believe some asshole tried to run us over," I blurted out, adrenaline still coursing through me.

Marko held me tighter while his guy started up the car, and we revved off quickly in the opposite direction from where the car had gone.

"Where to?" the guy called back.

"To the Estate," Marko replied before turning back to me.

"Whoever was shooting at us knew where we were and must have been following us, waiting for an opportunity to attack. Whether they were after you, me, or both of us, it doesn't matter. We are going to stay with my family where it will be safer."

Wait, what?

I wasn't keen on the idea of staying with Marko's family. They were strangers to me, and I felt uneasy. Right now, I needed to calm down and preferred doing that alone with Marko. Shaking like mad, I wasn't ready to engage with a bunch of strangers just yet.

"Are you sure we can't return to the apartment and go to see your family tomorrow as planned?" I asked, my voice quivering.

"The apartment's not safe, Melissa," he said.

"We don't know that!" I practically shouted, pulling away from him and putting some distance between us.

The little voice in my head chided me for being unreasonable, but fear and agitation were clouding my judgment. Everything had turned upside down, and now strangers were intruding into my life, pushing me into unfamiliar territory. It felt overwhelming, and rationality seemed out of reach.

"Someone just tried to run you over. They must have had some way of tracking us to find you, or we were being followed and didn't realise before, so we can't return to the apartment. We are going to my family's estate, and you will stay there with me until this situation is over," he said, his voice filled with barely contained fury.

I stared at him, the charming, sexy nerd I had met seeming to vanish before my eyes, replaced by a hardened and dangerous man. A lump formed in my throat, a sudden fear gripping me. What did I really know about Marko? Sure, he had claimed he had a code against hurting women, but what if that was all just talk?

I never truly considered him a threat, but now doubts crept in.

"Can I trust him?" I asked myself, biting my lip nervously. Deep down, I wanted to believe I could, but then the question extended to his family. Did they share the same principles? And who did he think he was, telling me what to do? Just because we had been intimate that didn't mean he could dictate my decisions. Annoyance bubbled up inside me, overtaking my momentary fear.

"I want to go to a hotel," I said, moving away from his side.

"We're going to my home," he replied firmly.

"No! I'm going to a hotel, drop me off at a hotel!" I practically shouted as anger took over rationality.

"Melissa, be reasonable. We've discussed this already. It's not safe," he pleaded, grabbing my hand.

"I'll check in under a different name. Nobody will know I'm there," I replied.

A muscle in his jaw twitched and I could almost hear the grinding of his teeth as he fought to remain calm.

"You're coming home with me!" he stated.

"You don't get to tell me what to do!" I shouted.

Marko went completely still, his intense gaze boring into me. You could cut the air with a knife. The waves of tension coming off him made me feel claustrophobic. Oh shit! I gulped, my palms beginning to sweat as I returned his gaze while desperately trying to hide the fear bubbling up inside me.

Marko must have noticed because I could see the

moment he realised he was frightening me. His demeanour shifted, and a wave of concern washed over his features as he seemed to deflate in on himself.

"Shit," he said, raking his hand through his hair before taking a deep breath.

"I didn't mean to scare you, Melissa," he murmured quietly.

My heart raced and I couldn't meet his eyes, unsure what to think.

"Look at me, sweetheart," he pleaded, scooting closer and gently tilting my chin up.

Biting my lip, I slowly let my eyes meet his intense gaze.

"I know you are feeling overwhelmed right now, but you have nothing to fear from me, Melissa. I've told you that already, and I meant it. I'm not angry with you, just frustrated over the whole situation," he said.

Reaching into his pocket, he pulled out a small knife. My eyes widened as he flicked it open. What was he doing?

"Please trust me?" he whispered, his tone beseeching.

Biting my lip, I nodded even as my stomach churned with worry.

"When I was a kid, my brothers, and a couple of friends, formed a brotherhood of our own, which we called the Bratva Blood Brothers. Each of us took a blood oath, vowing to always protect each other and our families, especially the females," he told me, nicking his thumb with the blade.

Lifting my hand, I winced as he did the same to mine, then pressed our thumbs together.

"I'm making a vow to you, Melissa, to always protect you. I will never hurt you. I swear that."

The intensity in his eyes and words sent shivers of lust straight to my core. All the fight left me and I swear he stole a piece of my heart in that moment. Chewing on my lip, I was at a loss for words as he continued.

"This whole thing has got me worried for your safety. We've only just met, but I already know that you are special to me. I'm terrified of how close I came to losing you twice now, before we've even had time to get to know one another properly, and I can't let anything happen to you. I need to keep you safe. Please let me," he pleaded, and I could see the conviction in his eyes.

I believed him, and I was in danger, so why was I fighting with him when all he wanted to do was keep me safe? Besides, the blood oath which some might find extreme was actually a huge turn on for me. Nobody had ever made me feel so special that they would vow to protect me in such a way.

"Please come and stay with me at my family's estate. We have security there. It will be the safest place for you. Even if you checked into a hotel under a different name, we don't know that they won't find you. They could still have someone following us, but even if they do, they won't be able to get to you at the Estate. Not with the level of security we have. I need to keep you safe. Please, Melissa?" he pleaded, leaning his forehead against mine.

Well, heck! How was a girl to resist?

Sighing heavily, I moved my head back so I could look into his eyes.

Although I would have preferred staying at a hotel rather than a house filled with strangers, especially criminal ones, I knew Marko was right once again. The flat was no longer safe, my home was destroyed, and I had nowhere else to go. If the MP's guys found me tonight, Marko was correct—they could easily track me down at a hotel.

My body trembled with fear at the thought. In the past two days, I'd been robbed, had a knife thrown at me, my home blown up in a gas explosion, and now almost run over. I was in way over my head. I needed protection and help if I was going to take down the MP before he had the chance to kill me. It made sense to agree.

Besides, Marko's proximity was weakening my resistance. The idea of staying anywhere with him was becoming more and more appealing as I gazed into those intense eyes and felt his breath on my face. Decision made, I nodded.

"Alright," I said, and he leaned down, pressing a kiss to my mouth.

"Thank you, sweetheart," he said, sounding relieved.

"But please ask me in the future before you make decisions concerning me," I told him firmly.

It was becoming evident that Marko could easily wrap me around his little finger, but I still needed to retain some of my autonomy. Although I had to admit, there were times when I felt having somebody to make decisions with, or even have help take over some of life's decisions, would be nice. Just not all of them. I was far too independent to submit completely to someone else making every decision for me.

"Yes, honey. I will," he said before kissing me deeply, that talented tongue of his chasing all my concerns away.

His phone vibrating between us a second later had us reluctantly pulling apart. Marko answered it and I could hear a man on the other end, his voice authoritative.

"I heard what happened. Bring her in now!" the man demanded.

"We're on our way," Marko responded.

"Good. It's the safest place for her, and I want everyone here until we sort this out. I spoke to Simpson. The bastard said his contacts told him that the person behind the new attacks against us is the MP, so I guess we can safely say we have a mutual enemy," the man instructed.

"I agree. The MP has gone too far. He's attacking our family and trying to kill my woman. He needs to be dealt with, and soon," Marko replied, fury lacing his voice once again.

"He will be!"

I barely registered the man's reply before he hung up because my mind was stuck on two specific words: "my woman". It seemed a bit soon for Marko to be getting possessive, yet I couldn't help liking the idea.

"Your woman?" I asked, raising my eyebrows in question, a small smile playing on my lips.

"Well, I would like to think that after what we did earlier and our date today, that you might… that we might…" he said, looking more flustered and embarrassed than I had ever seen him before. Seeing him so vulnerable, with his hand raking through his hair and his words trailing off, made my heart clench and a lump form in my throat. I cleared my throat.

"Might?" I prompted, my voice sounding breathy even to my ears.

Mr Sexy Nerd gulped hard, which only made him more endearing and I held my breath, awaiting his response.

"I like you, Melissa. I like you a lot, and I was hoping you might like me too," he said, less flustered this time but no less vulnerable.

I grinned. There really was no resisting this man.

"Yes, I do."

He grinned back before leaning in to reward me with a smouldering kiss.

CHAPTER 16
MARKO

LATER THAT SAME NIGHT – GETTING
ACQUAINTED

Miki was waiting outside the house for us with Ash, Romi, and Vlad when we arrived. I took in the size of the males as if I had never seen them before; they certainly looked intimidating, and I hoped the welcome party didn't scare Melissa off.

We stopped and climbed out. I slipped an arm around Melissa's shoulders, hoping to reassure her but also as a show of possession as I led her over.

"Melissa, these are my brothers, Miki and Ash, my cousin, Romi, and our good friend, and Miki's bodyguard, Vlad," I introduced them.

"You've already met my bodyguard, Trigger," I said, gesturing towards him as he retrieved her bags from the car.

They each smiled at her, and she seemed to relax. I was thankful for that because I wanted her to feel comfortable with my family and in our house, her new home. She might have thought it was just a temporary arrangement, but it would be a permanent one if I had my way. I inwardly smirked at myself. Miki was right, I was as bad as him and Ash. They both fell hard and fast for their women, and those women were now their wives and pregnant. It looked like I was falling just as hard and fast.

I stole a furtive glance at Melissa beside me as we walked towards the house, wondering if she had any idea what I was thinking and how she would feel about it if she did. A fleeting image of her in a wedding dress and then holding a baby also crossed my mind, and I pushed them quickly aside. Hmm, yep, I was definitely following in my brothers' footsteps.

However, one step at a time, I told myself; we had an enemy to deal with before I could think about a real future with my sexy cat burglar.

"It's lovely to meet you, Melissa, Marko has told me a lot about you, but I know there is still much to discuss. However, you must be tired, so I would suggest you both retire for the night. We can meet again in the morning to talk things over," Miki said, turning and gesturing for us to head inside.

As I led my Little Miss Pouty Lips into my home for the first time, all I could think about was getting her alone.

Our afternoon and evening together had been perfect, right up until we were nearly run over. Despite that, I had been eagerly anticipating getting Melissa alone in my bed again. I wanted to keep her to myself a little longer, but after everything she'd been through lately, bringing her home was definitely the right call.

She would be safer here, surrounded by my family and security. Plus, this would give her a chance to get to know everyone better. If she was going to be a permanent part of my life, she needed to feel comfortable with them. With Gracie, Eilidh, and Sonia around, I knew they'd make her feel welcome.

For a moment, I considered taking her to a guest room so she could rest, but quickly dismissed the idea. I shouldn't just assume she'd want to come to my bed again. But I wanted her there, so I wasn't giving her another option. Besides, she'd been receptive of the idea of further play between us when we left the restaurant and I was sure that hadn't changed.

Opening the door to my suite, I pulled her inside, closed the door, and pounced.

Flicking my tongue across her lips made her open them to me, and I delved right in. Not giving her any time to even think about anything else, as I claimed her mouth in a deep kiss.

When she kissed me back with as much gusto, confirming she wanted me as much as I did her, I was bloody elated. Our tongues tangled together in a now familiar battle for domination, which we both seemed to enjoy so much. We were left panting hard when we finally came up for air, staring at each other, and I knew the lust in her eyes mirrored mine.

Need consumed me and I pulled off her new top and

jeans frantically, I knew she'd been second guessing us earlier and I was afraid to give her time to change her mind again. I kissed her mouth, then her jaw, and down her neck before pulling back to take in her new lingerie. The dark pink lacy pieces covering her were gorgeous but needed to be off. I tugged her knickers down, and she stepped out of them for me. Then I grabbed her breasts and squeezed, feeling the lace against my skin before I reached around and unclipped her bra, tossing it aside.

After kissing her long and hard, I walked her backward to my bed and pushed her onto it. I stared down at her in awe for a second, unable to move as I took in the sight before me. My mouth was suddenly dry, and I licked my lips. Wow! That was the only thought in my head. Nothing else. I seemed suddenly incapable of forming a coherent thought other than, wow!

She reached for me with a little giggle, and I snapped out of my fugue-like state, stripping out of my clothes so quickly I almost tripped myself up as I pulled off my jeans. I jumped on the bed beside her, making her gasp. She giggled again at my obvious enthusiasm, but I cut it off abruptly as I claimed her lips in another searing kiss.

She tasted so good that I couldn't stop a groan of pleasure.

Pushing open her thighs with my knee, I positioned myself between them then took her nipple in my mouth and sucked hard, giving it a little nip as I did. She squealed at the slight pain before I flicked my tongue over her, soothing it better, then did the same to her other one.

Alternating between each boob, sucking and licking, I paid them both plenty of attention. After all, I didn't want either to feel left out. What could I say? I was a boob man, and hers were gorgeous. My hands squeezed them, kneading them gently as I sucked on her nipples.

Little Miss Pouty Lips' moans of delight went straight to my cock, which throbbed hard in response, desperate to get in on the action.

Down, boy! Not yet. It wanted me to take her hard and fast, but I was determined instead to drag our pleasure out. As I kissed her, I reached into the drawer beside my bed and retrieved a condom.

Dipping my head back down to her lovely breasts, I spent a good amount of time enjoying them further, pinching, licking, and sucking them as she arched towards me, holding my head to her, loving the attention I was giving.

But as much as I loved playing with them, soon it wasn't enough for either of us.

"Please, Marko," she pleaded.

I'd tortured us both long enough. Reaching between us, I rubbed her tight little nub. Her sex was wet and swollen for me already and I breached her with a finger, thrusting twice before adding another, then another. She was so tight, but soon I felt her hot channel relaxing around my fingers, giving way to their intrusion.

My cock throbbed painfully, and I couldn't wait any longer.

Sitting back, I gloved up, lined myself at her entrance, and surged forward.

"Fuck!" I shouted as I drove into her in one swift movement, hard and deep, right to the hilt.

Melissa wrapped her thighs around me, taking me deeper as I continued to pound into her relentlessly, grinding against her and circling my hips slightly at the end of each stroke. She was moaning and gasping, chanting my name against my lips as I kissed her.

"Yes!" she screamed as I pounded into her, my balls hitting her bottom with every inward thrust.

The little sounds she made were so hot, and I knew I couldn't hold out much longer, but I needed to make her come first. Her pleasure was even more important to me than my own. Increasing my efforts, I rubbed and pinched her clit. My tongue delved between her beautiful pouty lips, and I fucked her with it the way I was fucking her with my cock.

Melissa's whole body shook as she neared her climax. The sensation of her clenching tightly around me made me almost come there and then but I managed to hold off.

"Marko!" she cried tensing as she came hard.

Her words became incoherent mutterings as I continued to thrust hard, dragging out her release while I chased my own.

A couple more thrusts and I finally let myself go. My vision whitened and my back arched as wave after wave of pleasure hit me.

Unwilling to let her go yet, I held myself inside her,

savouring the feel of her wrapped around me as we both struggled to bring our breathing back to normal.

Fuck! I'd thought earlier had been the best sex I'd ever had, but hell, that just beat it. Dear god, I hadn't thought it could get any better.

My arms shook with the effort to hold myself over her without crushing her, and finally I forced myself to move. Rolling over, I turned her so I could spoon her and wrapped my arm around her waist, pulling her close.

"That was fantastic, Melissa," I whispered in her ear, nipping at the lobe.

"I…" Biting my tongue, I stopped myself from saying anything more when I realised I had been about to confess my feelings. There was no denying it, I was well and truly head over heels for this woman, but it was far too soon to tell her that. I wouldn't risk scaring her off.

Slow down! I chided myself. Little Miss Pouty Lips would be staying here, and we'd be spending a lot of time together. There would be plenty of time to work my charm on her and ensure she fell for me just as hard as I had for her.

Glad she was facing away from me; I closed my eyes and shook my head. It seemed I really was like my brothers after all, and I knew they'd enjoy teasing me about the fact soon enough.

Drawn to her like a magnet, I nuzzled her neck, kissing and nipping lightly on the skin. Melissa shivered and moaned, pushing her sweet bottom against me. I grinned, delighted with her reaction. She rubbed herself against me, gasping, as I licked my way up her neck and sucked her lobe into my mouth. And that was all it took for me to get hard again.

We should have been resting. She needed her sleep, I told myself, but the thought was fleeting as she pulled my arm down from her waist and between her legs, opening them for me.

She might indeed need rest, but she obviously needed something else, more and, of course, I couldn't possibly deny her.

Smirking at the thought, I let my fingers explore her more leisurely this time. It was going to be a long night. Hell yeah!

CHAPTER 17
MELISSA

SUNDAY MORNING – TIME TO MAKE
PLANS

Someone was nuzzling my neck and kissing me, and it was bliss. Smiling, I cracked open my eyes.

"Morning, beautiful," Marko said, leaning over me with a sexy grin. I enjoyed waking up to him.

"Time to get up. We need to head down for breakfast. Everyone wants to meet you, then we will need to spend the morning, or possibly the rest of the day, making plans with Miki," he said.

"I'll take a quick shower, then you can," he told me before hurrying off towards the bathroom, but not before I had time to admire his muscular back and tight bum.

That was a sight I wouldn't mind seeing on a regular basis.

I grinned as I jumped out of bed in search of clothes.

A short while later, Marko came out of the bathroom, wearing nothing but a towel wrapped around his waist. I salivated at the sight of those muscular shoulders and sexy abs of his. My god, my Mr Sexy Nerd was built!

I watched him open-mouthed as he walked past me to the wardrobe. He dropped the towel and pulled on some jeans, and I stared with undisguised lust, my gaze travelling up his legs, across his sexy ass, and over his back. My eyes took every inch of him, thoroughly enjoying the view, and I wished we could return to bed, but I knew that we had to meet with the others.

I openly ogled him, licking my lips. My gaze zoned in on the gorgeous tattoo on his left shoulder, which I stared at with curiosity. It was a six-inch Celtic cross with an eight-point star, which I immediately realised was the Bratva symbol, in the round centre forming the middle point. A scroll ribbon was wrapped three times around its length with some words written inside. It was beautiful, just like him. I made a mental note to ask him what the words meant later.

Marko chuckled, and I looked up to see I had been caught checking him out yet again. I would usually feel embarrassed if some guy saw me checking him out so thoroughly, but not with Marko. I smirked and blew him a kiss instead before turning and running into the bathroom, giggling as he tried to grab me.

When we got to the dining room, Marko introduced me to everyone, and I could hear the pride in his voice as he did so, which melted my heart toward him even further.

"It's lovely to meet you, Melissa," Eilidh said with a warm smile.

"Hey there, Melissa, nice to meet you," Gracie said.

"Hi, Melissa, welcome to the mad, bad, world of the Rominov's," Sonia said with a huge grin.

Nonna kissed both of my cheeks, then pinched them between her fingers like I was five or something. "Bella!" she exclaimed.

"Grazie mille," I replied in Italian.

Nonna's face lit up in delight and she clasped a hand to her chest.

"Parli Italiano?"

"Si, ho vissuto in Italia con i miei genitori per un po'," I replied.

"You lived in Italy with your parents for a while? Well, you must tell me all about it later. For now, eat," she said, leading me towards a huge breakfast buffet.

"You've made a friend for life there," Marko whispered, and I chuckled.

As we sat down to eat, I couldn't help overhearing Gracie and Sonia chatting.

"Did you say you wrote books, Gracie?" I asked, grinning.

"Yes, are you a reader?" she asked shyly.

"I like romance," I said.

"Hell yeah! Join the club," Eilidh said, grinning across the table at me.

"Gracie writes some of the best and smuttiest dark contemporary romance books I've ever read. Her book boyfriends are amazing," Sonia replied, wiggling her eyebrows at me.

"Hey!" several disgruntled male voices shouted in unison, and I laughed as Gracie practically choked on her bacon, Sonia's eyebrows rose almost into her hairline, and Eilidh's grin froze in place as they all remembered that we weren't alone.

"Of course, we each have our own men who'd rival any book boyfriend," Sonia said pointedly, winking at me.

"Good save," Romi said from beside her as he leaned down to kiss her soundly.

"Just reminding you of that fact," he said when he broke off, leaving her gasping for air and swooning.

Miki followed suit, kissing Eilidh in a way that made me blush. Oh, my, that man was intense! And so handsome. If I wasn't falling fast and hard for Marko, and if Miki wasn't already attached, I might just be crushing over him big time. I mean, wow!

"I don't need to remind Gracie of anything. I'm her inspiration," Ash said, grinning widely and waggling his eyebrows.

Everyone laughed as Gracie simply shook her head and chuckled at his antics.

Some good-hearted ribbing followed and by the time breakfast was over, my cheeks ached from all the laughing we'd done. Marko's family were funny and full of life and laughter. Not at all like I expected a Bratva family to be. My concerns about staying with a family of criminals had all been for nothing it seemed, and I quickly felt relaxed with them.

It was great that all of us women, even Nonna

apparently, shared a love of reading and especially romance. I was genuinely excited to hear that Gracie was a romance author herself and couldn't wait to read her books.

After breakfast, the ladies headed off to work, and the men headed to Miki's office.

"We'll be there in a minute," Marko told them as they left.

Pulling me aside, he wrapped his arms around me.

"What about me? Do I rival your book boyfriends?" he asked, grinning.

"Oh, you are way better than any of them," I reassured him with a chuckle.

"Right answer," he said, before kissing me so thoroughly my toes curled.

When he eventually let me up for air, I was panting hard and my whole body felt like a live wire. But he wasn't finished. Not by a long shot. Pressing me hard against the wall, his hand loosely around my throat, he kissed me once more.

While his tongue assaulted my mouth, his hands slipped into my leggings and rubbed my sweet spot. Lord, the things this man could do to me. Within minutes, I was bucking against his hand and crying into his mouth, and I swear I saw stars when my release came hard. My knees wobbled and if it wasn't for his body pressing so close to mine, I would have crumbled to the floor.

"That was so good!" I panted against his neck.

"Just making sure you have a comparison for future reference," he chuckled, sounding very proud of himself.

"Whenever you're reading, honey, let me know if there is any scene you want to try out and I'll be only too happy to oblige and show you just how much better I am to any fictional male," he said with a wicked grin and a wink.

My cheeks were on fire with all the delicious possibilities those words conjured up, and I was still giggling at my thoughts as we entered Miki's office.

Miki turned towards me, and his raised eyebrows and smirk told me he knew what we'd been up to. I cleared my throat and squirmed under his scrutiny until Marko stepped in to save me from further embarrassment.

"Melissa, meet Luca, one of our men and a close family friend," Marko said, introducing me to the new guy standing beside Miki.

"Pleased to meet you, Melissa," Luca said with a wink.

Marko huffed loudly and stepped between us.

"Enough of that. Keep your charms to yourself," he snapped at Luca.

"Oh, you've got it as bad as the rest of them," Luca replied, laughing.

"How the mighty fall. Isn't that what you said to me once, Marko?" Miki said, chuckling as Marko huffed again.

My embarrassment forgotten, I bit back a grin as I watched Marko squirm under the scrutiny of the two men. My heart did a little flip as Marko turned and winked at me.

"If you two have had your fun, shall we get started?" he said, leading me to where the others were seated around a large conference table.

Obviously, Marko had told Miki about me, but I wasn't sure what the others knew, so when he asked me to tell them all about myself, I didn't hold back.

As I spoke, I noticed that they all reacted in some small way to Mathieson's name when I told them how we were connected. However, none of their anger seemed directed at me, so I felt more relaxed.

Now that I had spent time with the family, I wasn't as worried about working with them anymore. So, I was being candid because I needed to build trust with these men. First, so that we could work together to bring the MP down, and second, because if Marko and I were to have any kind of actual future together, then I wanted to be accepted among his family and friends.

"Marko has told me what Mathieson did to your family and your friends, and I am sorry about that. I realise that he is missing and that it likely means you guys had something to do with it and he is likely dead. I just want you to know I understand why you would have felt it necessary to deal with him. His letter clearly said he was not a good man, and I believe that. I didn't know him, and I am glad, as he is not the type of person I would want anything to do with. The same can be said for my so-called uncle. The MP obviously doesn't want to know me, and I sure as hell don't want to know him, so whatever we need to do to ensure the safety of your family as well as myself, I'm up for that!" I said, finishing my speech in a rush.

The guys all stared at me. I think I shocked them a bit with just how candid I'd been, but I could see that I had done the right thing when each of them smiled at me.

"Glad you're working with us, Melissa. We'll do whatever it takes to destroy the MP and end his barbaric practices — for his victims and for the safety of our family, which now includes you," Miki said, his wide smile radiating warmth.

I returned the smile, a wave of happiness washing over me. Miki, as the Pakhan and head of the family, had welcomed me into their fold, and it was a relief to shed my feelings of isolation.

As we pored over the microchip and photographs, I scrutinised their reactions closely, hoping my trust in them was well-placed. These men were formidable, after all, their histories likely marred by acts of torture and murder. Yet, Marko had assured me of their code: they spared women and children, reserving violence only for those who directly threatened them and only as a last resort. I desperately wanted to believe that their principles were genuine.

The disgust on their faces was palpable. Each grimace and sharp intake of breath spoke volumes. The images of women in distress hit them hardest. Ash, visibly shaken, clenched and unclenched his fists, while Romi steadied him with a hand on his shoulder. Their reactions reassured me—-these were not men who took pleasure in inflicting pain.

The urgency to dismantle the MP's operation surged within me. This wasn't just about my safety or that of this family; it was about stopping his abhorrent practices for good.

Marko had hacked into the MP's security system, revealing the extent of his paranoia. With the multiple layers of security around the rooms where Mathieson's letter claimed the MP kept his most sensitive information; our task was daunting. I leaned on the skills my father had taught me, outlining how they could help us uncover the hidden evidence. Their approval bolstered my confidence; maybe, just maybe, I could meet their expectations.

CHAPTER 18
MARKO

SUNDAY MORNING – PLANNING A HEIST

Breakfast went off without a hitch, and by lunchtime, Melissa already felt like one of us. I had been wary about how the others would react to her being Aiden Mathieson's daughter—our former enemy whom we had taken down—but to my surprise, they embraced her almost immediately.

My little cat burglar's passionate speech about the arsehole and the MP did wonders to ease any lingering tension. Everyone seemed to relax around her, and she, in turn, appeared more comfortable with us. Miki's approving nod to me confirmed she was now accepted as family, which was a reassuring moment.

Regardless of our personal dynamics, Melissa now had the protection of both my family and the Bratva. That assurance meant everything in our dark world.

We spent the morning analysing the intelligence

Melissa had dug up on the MP, debating how her skills could help us lock down the evidence we needed for a solid case against him. Miki was livid about the recent attack on the poker game, and he had every right to be. We all felt the urgency to stop the MP before he caused more damage.

Cowardice wasn't tolerated among us, and the MP epitomised it, hiding in the shadows instead of facing us head-on. These vile hunts had to be stopped. Taking him down wasn't just about justice for the attacks on my family and Glowacki's—it was about ending his despicable practices once and for all.

Miki had tightened the noose around Nigel Simpson's neck, and Simpson confirmed that the MP was indeed behind the attacks on our businesses. The slimy weasel could have warned us but chose not to. To me, that was another nail in the untrustworthy bastard's coffin.

Simpson wasn't the go-between, but the rumour mill he had access to had clued him in on the situation. Or so he claimed. I didn't believe a word out of the man's mouth. Just thinking about him, even hearing his name, sent shivers of disgust down my spine. I'd seen those bloody surveillance tapes of him with those young, barely legal men too many times.

Eilidh joined us after lunch to help with the plans. When I brought up the topic of Simpson's imminent death, she shook her head. "We should keep him around, Marko."

I frowned. "He's a liability, Eilidh. Why keep the bastard alive?"

She met my gaze steadily.

"Simpson might still have useful information and he's the only one with an ear to the ground in the places we need it. We are still looking for more information on the human trafficking. Someone took over that operation before we could get to the other girls. This guy rubs us all up the wrong way, I know, but I don't think he can be underestimated. I believe there is more to the man than we know and I, for one, want to find out what. If he knows anything about the trafficking or can help us with any further information about the MP, then we still need him. The man will get his comeuppance, but we need to be smart about this. Let's use him while we can and wait until we finish with this MP first before you plan the guy's demise," Eilidh said.

"I agree there is more to him than we know, and that's why I think we should end him sooner rather than later. He can't be trusted. Anyway, he wasn't exactly forthcoming with the information about the MP. In fact, he made sure not to reveal what he knew," I replied unable to keep the annoyance out of my voice.

"That won't happen again. He's been told I expect regular updates on everything he finds out from now on. The guy knows if he fails me again, I'll end him immediately," Miki said.

"Fine," I mumbled. I still wasn't happy about letting the bastard breathe for even a second longer, but it was Miki's decision as pakhan, so I let it go.

The afternoon dragged on as we hashed out ideas, and

I found myself admiring Melissa's sharp mind and being impressed by her invaluable knowledge.

The MP's security system was top-notch, and he had a large security presence at his home. Between that and his personal bodyguards, getting the information we needed seemed nearly impossible. Yet, with Melissa's help, it felt doable.

"It won't be easy. We need a way in and out, some sort of distraction to keep the MP and his security team out of the way, a thorough plan, perfect timing, and plenty of luck to pull this off," Melissa stated, and despite the way she worried at her bottom lip with her teeth, I could sense her excitement building at the prospect of committing this heist.

Little Miss Pouty Lips had told me she had given up her criminal lifestyle and was looking for a quieter life, yet I doubted she realised just how much she appeared to relish the challenge and danger it presented. Her reaction gave me hope that once this was all over, the dangerous element of life with a Bratva man might not put her off staying with me.

Of course, I was running a head of myself again, but I couldn't seem to help it. I really was just as impetuous as the rest of my family, and I didn't care. Besides, it worked out for my brothers and Romi, so why not me?

"Oh, and an inside man!" she added, bringing my wandering thoughts back to the task at hand.

"Thankfully, we'd already thought of that," Ash replied.

"That's where you come in, Luca. You will be our inside man," Miki told his best friend, clapping him on the back as Luca rolled his eyes. I chuckled as I could almost see him thinking, "Here we go again!"

As Miki's best friend, Luca was well accustomed to Miki thrusting him into unexpected situations. He had always been Miki's go-to whenever he really needed someone he could rely on to get the job done and remain calm about it. Luca was one of those guys who not only exuded a calm confidence but could also ooze charm when he wanted to, making him great in any situation. Those traits were exactly why we had him oversee all of our entertainment venues.

"How exactly am I going to become the inside man?" Luca asked.

It was Ash who answered. "After talking to Anton about our most recent troubles, I learned that he had provided extra security for several MPs, including Timothy Evans-Hughes, at a recent political event. The MP had been impressed and had said he would be in touch should he need extra bodyguards in the future."

"So, after some gentle persuasion from us, one of the MP's personal bodyguards quit yesterday. The MP contacted Anton this morning as we'd hoped, and we arranged for you to go be his replacement," Miki said, slapping Luca on the back.

"Lucky me!" he replied, rolling his eyes again while the rest of us chuckled at the long suffering expression he wore.

"How long is this likely to take?" he asked.

"A few weeks at most. Hopefully less. We need to get him to trust you, but I don't want things to drag on too long. The sooner we can deal with this the better. I'll get Sonia and some of the staff to pick up the slack for you in your usual role in the meantime," Miki replied.

Melissa's brow creased. "Why not just blackmail an existing bodyguard to help us?"

"Blackmail is useful, but you can't ever fully trust a person who is being blackmailed to co-operate. Whenever possible, having our own man on the inside whom we could trust is a far better option. Luca will start tomorrow," Miki replied.

"Well, setting that up was fast work," Melissa said, the admiration in her voice clear.

Miki winked at her. "Our father was a great planner and strategist, and I do my best to emulate him."

"You are fantastic at making plans, baby, but Luca is going to need to get himself established and become a trusted employee quickly in order for him to obtain the security information we'll need for the heist. How are you planning on making that happen?" Eilidh asked, sidling up to Miki, who hugged her close and kissed the top of her head.

"No idea, but if anyone can figure that out, it's Luca," he replied, looking at the poor guy.

"Wonderful," Luca mumbled, and I couldn't help but smirk. Poor Luca was always being landed in trouble by his best friend. But Miki was right. Luca could charm the pants off anyone, so if there was any way to endear himself quickly to the MP, he'd find it.

"As to the distraction, for getting in and out, I may know the perfect thing," Miki said, a slow smile spreading over his face before he disappeared outside.

A short while later, Miki returned, sporting a huge grin.

"I just checked with a friend of ours, Marcie Matthews owns an events company. She has worked for us several times and last year helped with the opening of our new nightclub, Glitz. However, she inadvertently became double-booked on the night because another event she had been organising for a local MP had needed to be brought forward," he explained for Melissa's benefit.

"Anyway, Sonia had mentioned Marcie was doing another event for him soon. So, I checked with Marcie and as luck would have it she was in charge of another of his political events at his country estate soon and the MP in question is…"

"Drum roll please," Miki said, looking at Ash.

Chuckling, Ash obliged with a drum roll on the desktop.

"None other than Timothy Evans-Hughes."

Cheers filled the room.

"So, that gives us our inside man, and the event itself should provide the distraction, keeping the MP and most of his security busy. Unfortunately, it is in three weeks," Miki stated.

What?

"Melissa, it that enough time?" I asked, concerned that it wouldn't be.

She paused before answering, and I could see the wheels turning in her head as she thought everything through. Finally, she smiled.

"We'll have to make it work!"

CHAPTER 19
MELISSA

SUNDAY AFTERNOON – THE PLAN TAKES SHAPE

Once we had a time frame, we dived into the work with determination. Within a few hours, we had laid the foundation of our plan. With three weeks to execute it, the timeline was tight but manageable.

We meticulously dissected each layer of the MP's security. The most challenging part of the operation would be bypassing the security code for his secure rooms. He changed it every few days, and the keypad required his unique fingerprints. On top of that, a retinal scanner added another layer of complexity. That was where I would need to do the most work and rely heavily on my gymnastic background. This was going to be one tough mission.

"So, it's agreed. Melissa and I will go in together to do the heist in one of Marcie's vans. Luca's job will be to obtain a copy of the MP's prints, find out about staff levels, confirm all the security measures and get us into the house on the day. Hacking into the main security system during the heist and providing any codes will be my job. Miki will co-ordinate everything from here with Eilidh and the rest is up to Trigger and Vlad who will be in charge of distractions and escape routes," Marko said.

We all nodded our agreement.

"And I will ensure everything is business as usual here and cover any alibi's should they be required," Romi supplied.

"Great. We are getting there, folks," Miki said and I couldn't help admiring just how quickly he'd made things come together.

Relief filled me as I looked around the room of people who were helping me, feeling glad to be a part of this team. I enjoyed brainstorming with them, appreciating their input and the trust they had in each other. It was exactly what I needed. After finalising the main plan, Miki led us through multiple contingency plans, showcasing his strategic thoroughness. He reminded me of my dad—they would have got along well. I was sure my dad would have liked these guys.

To be honest, I quickly grew fond of them myself. They not only made me feel welcome, and a valued part of the team, but they also often deferred to me, recognising this was my area of expertise. That made me feel special. I noticed how often Marko looked impressed with me too, and, well, I had to admit, I liked that as well.

As the day wore on, I realised how much I had missed the excitement of making this sort of plan. I had thought I wanted a quiet life, but now I wasn't completely sure. While I still didn't want to be in regular danger, I finally admitted to myself that a truly quiet life, the kind I had been recently imagining, would be utterly boring.

Of course, now that I was involved with my Bratva man and his family—and there was no denying that I was indeed very much involved with both—I doubted my life would ever be that quiet again.

By the time we headed into the dining room to meet up with the other women for a late dinner, I was pleased with the results of the day's work, though somewhat exhausted. The chat was light-hearted with a lot of good-natured bantering, especially from the boys who took great pleasure in taunting Marko about finally coming out from behind his computer screens long enough to get himself a woman.

Being called his woman should have been annoying, but I found I was actually secretly thrilled. Not that I was going to admit that.

"It's early days. We've only just met, so it's a bit soon to be proclaiming me Marko's woman," I scoffed.

That just earned me a laugh, and a wink followed by the comment, "We'll see," from the man in question, while the others simply chuckled.

Gracie turned to me, her eyes sparkling, and her voice filled with amusement, "I said that too. My conviction lasted all of about an hour."

"That's because I'm better than any book boyfriend," Ash replied, winking at her.

Everyone burst into fits of laughter.

Romi turned to Sonia, "Hey, I thought I was?"

"You are too, honey!" she replied, rolling her eyes and patting his arm soothingly.

Miki simply glanced at Eilidh with his eyebrows raised.

She giggled.

"You too, babe!" she said before kissing him on the cheek. As he nodded his approval, his lips twitching as he fought to keep a straight face.

"So, we are all book boyfriend material," Ash said as all three of the men looked smugly at Marko, "the question is, are you?" he asked, chuckling.

"I'm pretty sure Marko can wipe the floor with the lot of you, if he wants."

The room filled with *oohs* and *ahhs* ay my statement and I couldn't help giggling at the smug look on Marko's face and the looks of mock offence on the others.

If anyone had told me just a few days ago, I would be sitting here joking around with members of the Russian mafia about them being better than book boyfriends, of all things, or how quickly I would find myself at ease with them, I would never have believed them.

"Sounds like a challenge, Marko," Sonia said tauntingly.

"I like a challenge," he replied, winking with a grin filled with wicked promise.

Oh, my! My heart fluttered and butterflies did a happy dance in my stomach.

"But are you up to it?" Miki asked, smirking.

Grinning, I leaned over and whispered as seductively as I could manage into Marko's ear, "Well, are you?"

"Oh yes, Little Miss Pouty Lips. Challenge accepted!" he stated loudly.

My cheeks flushed with heat and a rush of wetness dampened my knickers as the room filled with whoops and cheers and I wondered just what I'd got myself into.

CHAPTER 20
MARKO

"Challenge accepted," I said as whoops and cheers filled the room.

"Well, I'd better get started," I said, grinning wickedly as I hurried Melissa out of the room. The good natured taunts of my family rang in our ears all the way down the hall.

My family liked to rib me about being a nerd, but of course what they forgot about nerds is that we were well read and knowledgeable. I might be the youngest of my brothers and probably a little less experienced, but I knew my way around a woman's body and not from theory alone.

Although I had to admit, I had a sneaky peek or two at some books my sister and the other women read. Just for research purposes, of course. I loved my research, after all, and it paid to be thorough. So, I was more than aware of book boyfriends and their behaviour.

"Slow down, Romeo," Melissa giggled as I practically ran her upstairs.

"Oh no, honey. You issued me with a challenge, and I accepted. Besides, I never back down from a challenge. By the time I'm finished with you, you'll not only believe I'm the best book boyfriend you could dream up in the flesh, but you will be more than happy for everyone to know you're my woman," I purred.

Proving I could be better than any fictional male was going to be a piece of cake. I would have Melissa eating out of my hand and begging to be mine by morning so that nobody, not even her, would doubt that she was mine. Things were moving fast, but I was happy with that and I was going to do whatever it took to convince her we were right together.

Anyway, it wasn't as if we had met under normal circumstances and could date in the usual manner. Instead, we were forced into close proximity to ensure her safety, so I might as well take advantage of that. Full advantage!

The minute I opened the door to my rooms, I pulled her round and crowded her, one hand leaning on the doorframe above her head, the other gently stroking her cheek, as I leaned forward and kissed her just long enough for her to clock the position. *Book boyfriend position one*, I mentally ticked off from the list in my head.

Next, I closed the door, pushing her up against it, my hand lightly holding her throat as I kissed her thoroughly. *Book boyfriend position two – check.*

Melissa moaned into my mouth, and I couldn't contain the smug grin as I pulled back.

My Little Miss Pouty Lips had got the memo. She knew exactly what I was doing and giggled as I lifted her up and carried her into the bathroom, placing her onto the vanity top. Positioning her legs on either side of my hips, I grabbed her bum with one hand and the back of her head with another, grinding my erection into her core as I gave her another long, slow, lingering kiss. *Book boyfriend position three!*

Yeah, I was pretty sure I was nailing this book boyfriend thing.

Finally, I pulled away, panting hard, and stared into her eyes, happy to see the half-glazed look of lust which I knew mirrored my own.

With the basic positions done, I decided to up the ante.

Moving away just long enough to turn on the taps, I returned to kiss her as the bath filled. Trailing light kisses across her jaw and down her neck, my hands worked on removing her leggings.

The spot where her neck and shoulder met drew me in, and I slowly sucked on it as my hand slipped between us. Pushing aside the crotch of her underwear, I slid a finger into her.

"You're wet for me, babe," I said as I slowly thrust my finger back and forth inside her. She groaned in pleasure, and more wetness coated my fingers as I delved into her silky, slick channel.

Fuck, she felt so good. I wanted to be inside her, but I

was determined to make things slow and seductive and worship every inch of her.

Melissa's eyes widened as I licked my fingers clean of her juices.

After checking the temperature of the water, I stripped off the rest of her clothes. Worshiping every part of her body as I unveiled it, I interspersed light kisses with little licks and nips, delighting in her soft gasps and moans.

Satisfied I had kissed her from the top of her head to her toes, I stepped away, turned off the water in the tub, and stripped out of my own clothes.

Once naked, I returned to my place between her thighs and palmed her breasts while kissing her pouty lips. I rubbed her nipples between my fingers, then gently tugged. She gasped and pushed her breasts into my hands, and I squeezed them as I devoured her mouth.

Our tongues entwined, and I growled low in my throat. I loved her taste and the feel of those full, luscious lips of hers beneath mine.

While I played with her nipples, I slid a hand down her body, slipping it between her wet folds. She cried out, her hips thrusting upwards as my middle finger pushed inside.

"Marko," she moaned, as I added another finger, curling them slightly.

I slowly moved my fingers in and out of her, pressing my thumb against her clit with each inward stroke. Melissa panted and moaned and bucked her hips in an effort to make me speed up, but that wasn't the plan. I refused to be rushed and kept things slow and teasing.

"Please, Marko, I need to come," Melissa begged before I finally relented and built up speed.

The noises my Little Miss Pouty Lips made turned me on and my cock was rock hard by the time her breaths became faster and shallower. I fisted her hair, tugging her head back so I could gently nip that sweet spot where her neck and shoulders met. Her hips pushed up against my hand as she desperately tried to ride my finger as her climax built to a frenzy.

My heart pounded, and my cock throbbed painfully. She was so close. Her excitement made me want to come too. I wanted so badly to let my cock explode right now, but I wouldn't let that happen, not yet.

"Come for me, Melissa. Show me how much you love what I do to you," I demanded before taking her mouth again.

The sound of Melissa's scream as she broke apart for me was muffled by my kiss. It was the last straw; I couldn't take it any longer. Needing to be inside her, I removed my fingers, replacing them with the head of my cock. Rubbing myself back and forth, sliding my length through her slick folds, I groaned at the feel of her juices coating my shaft. She felt so good, too good, I had to squeeze myself, so I wouldn't spill my seed there and then.

As I took slow, steadying breaths, I gazed into her beautiful green eyes. The intensity of our connection amazed me. I was halfway in love with this woman despite only knowing her for a few days.

With a slight chuckle, I had to admit that, yes, I really was as mad as my brothers.

My eyes roamed over the beautiful woman in front of me, panting for breath, her gorgeous naked body slick with sweat. My heart swelled, knowing I was the reason for it. Me, the family nerd.

Little Miss Pouty Lips smiled up at me seductively, the smell of her arousal perfuming the air. Her hair was dishevelled, her pouty lips even fuller and pinker with my kisses, her eyes glazed with passion, and her shallow pants echoed around the room. Fuck, she truly was a sight to behold.

And mine. All mine!

Yes, it seemed that I was not only as mad as my brothers, but as possessive, too. Shaking my head, I chuckled at the thought, as I took her mouth in another demanding kiss.

Melissa shuddered and grabbed my cock.

"Enough, Marko, I need you inside me now. Please," she pleaded.

"Tell me you're mine first, Little Miss Pouty Lips," I said, smiling against her mouth.

Melissa pulled away from me, laughing. "Little Miss Pouty Lips?"

"Suits you, honey. These full pouty lips of yours drive me insane and make me think of so many delicious things I want you to do with them," I said, licking my own lips as my eyes zoomed in on her mouth. All the while, I continued torturing us both by rubbing my cock against her slit.

"Well, Mr Sexy Nerd, these pouty lips of mine will be more than glad to oblige you," she said, her eyes dancing with mirth.

"Mr Sexy Nerd?" I asked, laughing hard.

"Suits you, honey," she replied, copying my earlier words.

"I like it," I murmured against her mouth.

"However, before I can give you what you need, you need to give me what I need," I told her, allowing my length to breach her just a fraction and no more.

She pushed towards me, trying to take more of me, but I pulled away.

"Tell me you're mine, honey," I demanded.

"Only if you tell me you're mine first," she replied with a playful grin.

The little minx's eyes danced with mirth as she clasped her hand around my shaft, and I swear I saw stars flash behind my eyes at the feel of her touch.

"I'm yours." The words shot out of my mouth without conscious thought, and so quickly they were almost incoherent.

My sexy little cat burglar laughed at my response as her hand pumped my length, and I shuddered.

Leaning forward, she whispered in my ear.

"Say it again, Mr Sexy Nerd. Tell me you're mine." Her breathy voice sent shivers of pleasure down my spine that almost rivalled the pleasure of her hand on my cock.

Holy shit. I couldn't take it anymore, I needed to be inside her now.

"Melissa, I can't take much more. I'm yours. Tell me you're mine and let me show you how good we are together," I pleaded, my voice strained as I clung on desperately to the last shreds of my control, unwilling to come until I was buried deep inside her.

My breaths came out hard and fast as I looked into her eyes. I was used to being in control. How had she turned the tables on me so easily? I needed to flip things back again because I wasn't going to last a second longer at this rate.

My hand shot between us, and I plunged two fingers into her. She groaned, tilting her hips towards me. Matching the rhythm of her hand on my shaft, I pumped my fingers into her wetness. Grabbing the back of her head, I took her lips in a punishing kiss, only pulling away when we were both gasping for air.

"I'm yours, Marko," she cried, finally giving me the words I'd longed to hear as she came around my fingers.

While she rode her orgasm, I pulled her hand off me, shifted my hips into position, and slipped into her in one long stroke. She gasped and her pussy clamped down hard on my length.

"God, you feel so good, Melissa," I panted into her ear.

She was so tight, milking my shaft so well that my eyes rolled back in my head as I clung to her and came, following her into bliss.

As our breathing returned to normal, I stayed inside

her, holding her tight. It was not just that I didn't want to let her go, I couldn't. My legs were shaky, and my head was swimming from the climax of a lifetime. I'm not sure what it was about Melissa, but I couldn't get enough of her. We fit together like we were made to. Being in her arms excited me and yet also felt like home. I could definitely see my future with her.

As she nuzzled my neck, I pulled back to look at her.

"You turn me on like no other woman, Melissa. I like you a lot," I told her, brushing her lips gently with mine.

"I like you a lot too, Marko," she murmured before sucking my bottom lip.

Groaning, my cock jerked to attention again.

Uh, Uh!

While I would have loved to accommodate it and take her again, I saw the lines of exhaustion on her face that she tried to hide during dinner, so any further sexy time would have to wait.

"Hey," she squealed, then giggled as I lifted her up and lowered her into the bathtub.

Melissa reached for me obviously expecting me to join her, but I was determined to be a gentleman. The last few days were taking their toll on my woman, and I needed to take care of her. Like any book boyfriend would do. I chucked inwardly at how seriously I was taking this challenge.

"Relax and enjoy your bath. There will be plenty of time to bathe together in the future, tonight you need to relax and rest. I will see you when you're done," I told her, kissing the top of her head as she lay back and closed her eyes.

Her deep sigh of contentment made me smile as I slipped out of the bathroom.

After closing the door, I grabbed the box containing the gift I got her out of my jacket pocket and set about fixing it with a tiny tracker. Then I added another to her phone.

Ever since my sister Krissa was murdered, I made sure I could track all my family members through their phones. Lately, I'd been working on smaller devices and developed ones that could be fitted into jewellery. Now, whenever any woman in the family received a piece of jewellery, I ensured that it was embedded with a tiny tracker.

After Ash was abducted and his phone discarded, I extended this to watches and other jewellery for the guys too. I was even considering placing some trackers in their belts and tie pins and wherever else I could. Of course, they probably wouldn't like that, but I didn't plan on telling them. My family thought I was paranoid enough, and nosey. I wasn't. It was not as if I had been following their every move, listening in on private calls and stuff. The trackers were only used in emergencies.

Admittedly, they might have been right about me being paranoid when it came to the safety of my family, perhaps even obsessed. I couldn't help it. My family meant the world to me, and their safety was my biggest priority. My tattoo said '*Moya sem'ya eto vse*', which meant '*My family means everything.*'

So obsessed or not, I would continue to track them any way I could. If we had taken extra precautions before Kissa was murdered, if I had given her the watch I bought for her graduation before she went out that night, she might still be alive. The bastards who killed her had thrown her phone away when they grabbed her, but if she had been wearing the watch, I could have tracked her.

Ash blamed himself for being late to pick our sister up that night. I blamed myself for not being able to track her. I failed her, and I was determined not to fail anyone else. Nobody else would be taken or hurt on my watch if I could do anything about it.

Melissa returned to the bedroom a short time later, looking relaxed, sleepy, and sexy as hell. Climbing into bed beside her, I cuddled her close as we both drifted off to sleep wrapped in each other's arms.

CHAPTER 21
MELISSA

Snippets of memories of happier times with my parents floated through my head. Laughter rang out as instrumental music filled the air, and the smell of candy floss made my mouth water.

"Mummy, look!" I shouted, pointing to the carousel with brightly coloured horses. Grabbing her hand, I tugged her towards it. Her laughter blended with mine as we bobbed up and down on the horses and waved to my dad who watched us.

We next strolled down a quiet street in Rome, savouring gelato, our voices mingling with the sounds of the city. In Montreal, we were running through a park. Dad chased me, lifting me into the air and twirling me around as I giggled with delight.

Mum's voice called my name, and I turned to see her smiling as she crossed the street to collect me from school. She looked so beautiful, and my heart ached as she embraced me tightly, as she always did whenever we were apart.

Suddenly, my mind flashed to abseiling down the side of a building, dressed in black, a rush of adrenaline coursing through me as I saw my dad doing the same beside me.

Then, I watched my parents dance on a balcony under the stars, feeling blessed by their love and happiness.

But before long, things turned bad. A room appeared, reminiscent of the Opera Gallery in Monaco. Instead of art, the walls displayed family photographs, and the sculptures embodied memories of my parents.

No sooner had I registered that fact than the glass shattered unexpectedly, and the pictures curled at the edges as they were consumed by fire, turning to dust. Smouldering paper drifted down like confetti in hell, the heat becoming unbearable.

Panicked, I turned to my parents and watched in horror as their faces melted like wax, their features distorting into unrecognisable lumps.

"No, please! Don't leave me!" I cried, reaching out towards them, grasping desperately at emptiness.

Screams filled my ears. I covered them to drown out the sound, but it was relentless, piercing through my attempts to block it out.

"Melissa! Melissa, wake up, honey!"

The sound of Marko's voice eventually penetrated my subconsciousness, and I came awake with a start, my heart racing, my breathing harsh as tears ran down my face.

"It's okay, sweetheart. It was just a nightmare," Marko said, stroking my hair, as he held my trembling body as the last remnants of the nightmare faded.

Sniffing hard, I lay there and let him soothe me, his warm embrace comforting me as my breathing slowly returned to normal. That was the first nightmare I'd had since I was a child, and it was very disconcerting.

As my brain connected the dots, I knew what it meant. Everyone I cared for and everything we'd owned were nothing but dust. My memories had all been taken in the blink of an eye, and I was left alone.

Leaning back, I looked into Marko's eyes.

"I hate Mathieson for dragging me into his problems and the MP for blowing up my home. I need that bastard to pay," I said angrily.

"I know, Melissa, and we will make sure he does," Marko said, pulling me back into his chest.

My bottom lip trembled as I fought the urge to scream or cry again. Illness had taken both my parents, but the MP had taken my memories and for that he needed to be held accountable.

"Everything's gone, Marko," I said, sadness filling every word and tears threatening to spill despite my best efforts.

"No, honey. Only physical things have been destroyed. Your memories are still intact, buried inside. Nobody can ever take those away from you," he murmured against the top of my head and stroked my back.

"I feel so alone," I sniffed into his bare chest.

Tilting my head towards him, Marko gazed into my eyes.

"You are not alone, Melissa. Not anymore. You have me and I plan on being with you for as long as you'll let me. And you have my family, and together we will destroy the MP. Then after that, if you let me, I will help you relive some of those memories you have and even make some of our own," he said.

I gulped hard. Oh my, I was definitely falling for this guy.

"I'd like that," I said with a watery smile.

Marko's eyes lit up, burning with an intensity that made my heart hammer in my chest and my core damp.

It should have worried me that I was already halfway in love with Marko, we'd only just met after all, and he was part of a dangerous world that I'd vowed to leave behind, but it didn't. Not one bit.

In fact, I loved the idea of being with him. It seemed serendipitous that Marko had come into my life just when I was feeling so lonely and needed help. I wanted to see where this thing between us could go, and I was pleased that Marko felt the same.

Feeling safe and cocooned in his arms, I sighed and snuggled closer to him as he gently stroked my hair.

Of course, it wasn't long before having my hair stroked by Marko, led to thoughts of being stroked elsewhere. Being in his arms had calmed me after my nightmare, but the longer I lay there the more I became aware of the hard

172

planes of his body beneath me, and my fingers couldn't resist exploring them.

I might not be alone as such anymore, but the nightmare had brought home to me exactly what I had lost and the lingering desolation of that remained now I was awake. I needed to find a way past that.

"Sorry I woke you," I said to him. Not truly sorry. My fingers made slow circles over his bare pecks, my hands slipping lower towards his abs with every movement.

"No problem, sweetheart. Are you okay now?" he asked.

"No, I need to be comforted more after my nightmare. Maybe distraction would help," I smiled up at him, waggling my eyebrows suggestively.

A slow grin replaced the concern in his eyes.

"You do, huh? And exactly what did you have in mind?" he asked, his lips twitching in amusement.

"Well, I'm sure anyone who thinks he is better than any book boyfriend could come up with something," I replied wickedly.

"Oh, I'm sure I can find all sorts of ways to *comfort* you," he smirked.

"Prove it!" I challenged.

He laughed, rolling us over so quickly I squealed in surprise.

Then he was on me, claiming my mouth in a deep kiss. I kissed him back with as much enthusiasm. Our tongues tangled as we delved into one another, exploring every inch of each other's mouths only separating when finally forced to come up for air.

Marko's gaze scanned my body, his lips lifting in a sexy smirk as he looked at me. I could look into his gorgeous blue-grey eyes forever. Nobody had ever looked at me like that and it made me want to melt. Or come on the spot. My pussy spasmed, my lady parts practically humming for him.

The sheet that had covered us fell away as I straddled him, and I watched his eyes darken with lust at the sight of my bared boobs. Grabbing them, he squeezed, then sucked first on one nipple, then the other, lavishing both with the same amount of attention, as he always did.

I brought his head up again and kissed his mouth, before reaching between us and claiming the prize that was hardening nicely for me there.

Marko gasped into my mouth, and I smirked as I moved my hand back and forth, enjoying how he reacted to my touch. His laboured breathing egged me on, and I nipped his ear and kissed his neck before moving lower.

Determined to taste him, I continued to pump his cock as I slid down his body, kissing and licking him from his collarbone, and across his pecs, to down his gorgeous abs. I stopped to lap at his belly button and his panted breaths grew harsher.

Feeling like a sex goddess at how easily I could make this gorgeous male breathless, I smiled against his skin. When he bucked against my hand, I licked his hip bones that formed that sexy as hell V which led to the pleasure centre I couldn't wait to taste. My mouth watered at the thought, and I blew on the little hairs that pointed the way to my anticipated destination.

Marko groaned loudly, his breaths coming fast and harsh, and I grinned as I saw his hands on either side of his hips clutching the sheets tightly, as he fought to lie still and allow me my explorations. God, I loved playing with him.

Finally, I licked the little drop of pre-cum off the tip of the glorious member that had already rocked my world and ruined me for any other man. His hands shot to my head and fisted in my hair. I glanced up to see Marko staring at me through half-closed eyes with a look of raw need that took my breath away.

Watching him as he lay there, panting hard and fighting for control, sent a shiver of smug triumph through me. It delighted me that I was the woman making this gorgeous male feel that good. Smiling, I licked the length of him, and he shuddered before I took him into my mouth.

The slightly salty taste of him was appealing, and I wanted more of it. Sucking him deep, I cupped his balls and gave them a gentle squeeze as I moved my head up and down his length. He was just too big for me to take without gagging, so I clasped my hand around the bottom of his shaft and continued to pump it while I sucked.

"God, Mel, I can't last much longer. If you keep this up, I'm going to come," he panted, his jaw tight with the tension it took to keep from doing just that.

"Come, Marko. I want to taste you. You've tasted me; it's only fair," I said when he started to shake his head.

"Fair is fair," he replied, and suddenly my mouth was filled with his cum. I'd never swallowed before because in the past I'd never liked the taste of semen, but Marko's didn't bother me, and I sucked it down then lapped at his slit to clean him up.

"Phew, that was amazing, honey. In fact, it was the best blow job I've ever had. But I thought I was supposed to be *comforting* you," Marko said with a huge and very wicked grin as he grabbed me and pulled me up his body.

Positioning me over his face, I gasped as his tongue licked my slit.

Oh, my! I guessed My Sexy Nerd was about to return the favour.

My eyes rolled back in my head as Marko attacked me with relish. If I didn't know better, I would suspect him of trying to ensure that I would soon confirm that he was the best at going down on me than anyone else. I couldn't help but smirk at the thought. Oh baby, bring it on!

It didn't take long before I was gripping the headboard and riding his face like a feral thing. I was so close, just teetering on the edge of a release when Marko moved us so that he was lying on top of me.

I was about to protest, but he cut my words off, capturing my mouth again and adjusting his cock so that it lined up with my entrance. Holding himself there, he reined more kisses over my mouth, jaw and down my neck, making me shiver.

With one hand on my hips and the other at the back of my head, he held himself still, teasing me by rubbing his erection between my wet folds, pressing it against my clit briefly with each upward stroke.

Tilting my hips up, I silently begged for him to fill me, but he wasn't ready to oblige. Playing hard to get, he moved back, teasing me again and again, until I was a hot mess, writhing and moaning with pleasure beneath him.

God, this man did things to my body I never knew were possible and I couldn't get enough of my Mr Sexy Nerd. Grunts, groans and moans filled the room, and I vaguely wondered if anyone could hear us, but then realised I didn't care. Not right now. Later might be a different story, but I wasn't about to let any future embarrassment stop me from enjoying the present.

"Marko, you're killing me," I cried as he chuckled in my ear.

Mr sexy Nerd was playing a bloody tease, and he was relishing the role.

"Please, Marko," I groaned.

"What do you want Melissa? Tell me what you need?" he said, his voice strained with the tension of holding himself over me.

"You, Marko, inside me. Now!" I panted the words out loudly, practically screaming them.

Finally, I felt a nudge at my entrance.

"Yes!" I cried and tried to lift my hips, but he held me down.

Slowly, inch by inch, he entered me, taking his time

and staring at where our bodies joined with such a look of awe that I nearly came again from that alone.

"Please," I begged.

He pushed in further, finally seating himself inside me to the hilt, before slowly, achingly slowly, pulling back out, then suddenly slamming back into me.

"Oh, fuck."

"More, Marko, please," I begged, panting hard, lifting my legs, and wrapping them around his waist, pulling him closer.

"Fuck me!" I screamed against his neck, becoming frantic, as he teased me over and over, making me mad with need.

"Stop teasing. Please, Marko. Now!" I cried, smacking his bum in outrage at his teasing ways.

"Ow!" he cried out, laughing hard at my frustration.

I was so bloody horny I was near out of my mind with it and if he didn't give me what I needed right that second I was going to punch him upside the head.

"Oh, I never knew you were so violent," Marko chuckled, making me realise I must have said my threats aloud.

But he got the message, and his teasing finally ended.

Marko's movements sped up, his rhythm becoming almost punishing as his own need grew until all I could do was cling on as he pounded me into the bed so hard I wondered for a second if we were actually going to break it.

I watched my Mr Sexy Nerd as he held himself above

me. His muscles strained with tension, his skin glistened, and a small bead of sweat ran down the side of his face. I've no idea why, but I wanted to taste it. So, I did, I lifted my head up and licked it. He turned his face capturing my lips, and I pushed my tongue into his mouth. As usual, Marko quickly took over the kiss, fucking me with his tongue as he fucked me with his cock.

My nipples were being rubbed deliciously as our bodies slid together, sending sparks of electricity straight to my core. Marko groaned, and the sound vibrated right through his body and mine, connecting us both, making me quiver like a tuning fork.

It was as if with Marko, everything was heightened, all my senses more enhanced. If I wanted a distraction, he was certainly providing one. If I wanted comfort, this was anything but. There was nothing comfortable about the way he was fucking me. It was raw, hard, breathtaking, and primal, and I loved it. Seconds later, I exploded, my orgasm making my legs spasm and my vision white out.

But Marko wasn't finished. I lay there gasping for breath and soaring on the wings of my high as he continued to pound me hard, not letting up. I hadn't even come down when I realised my body was building up for another release. How the hell was that even possible? I'd never actually come with a man before, yet with Marko, I'd come every time he touched me. Multiple times, in fact.

My emotions were wrecked. I sobbed with pleasure as

he rammed into me, circling his hips slightly with every inward thrust.

Oh my god, how could anything be so good? How could anyone make me feel so amazing? My core clenched and milked his shaft hard. Marko's movements became jerky, then his whole body tensed. We both cried out as our bodies released together.

Unable to move, we clung to each other, savouring the feeling of him still buried deep as the waves of our pleasure slowly receded.

Before Marko, I had thought the sex I had with the few guys I had been with was okay, nothing great, but not bad either. However, Marko had shown me the error in my belief. Those guys had nothing on him.

The chemistry between us was special. This was not just lust or a crush, this went way deeper. In fact, I was sure I was already halfway in love with the guy.

"That was fantastic, Melissa," Marko said when our hearts had stopped racing and our breathing had returned to normal.

Shifting me off him, he tucked me into his side, and I snuggled close. We lay there and enjoyed the calm after our tempestuous love making.

A short while later, Marko broke the silence. Peering down at me, his eyes danced with mirth and his voice was laced with amusement as he asked, "Did I prove it? Am I better than any book boyfriend you could have?"

"Hell yeah!" I replied, laughing. "Although I'm not sure you can keep that up long term," I joked.

"Challenge accepted, honey," he whispered gently nipping my ear, his voice sultry and the Russian accent thicker than usual.

Licking my lips, I bit back a groan as my core clenched in response. Oh my, that accent was a panty melter for sure.

As he rolled on top of me, my eyes widened as I felt him getting hard again.

"Already? Seriously?" I asked unable to keep the awe from my tone.

"Unless you are too tired?" he whispered against my neck as he feathered kisses across my collarbone.

Tired? I was, and I knew we should both be getting some rest, but to hell with it. Rest could wait.

My body quivered in anticipation as I opened my legs in silent invitation. He accepted immediately, positioning himself between them and licking his way down my body. As his tongue lapped at me again, all I could think was, 'Oh my, he really is taking this *better than any book boyfriend challenge* seriously.' My toes curled, and I smiled wickedly at that thought. I was going to enjoy this.

CHAPTER 22
MARKO

A loud snore woke me. I must have dozed off lounging in the chair in my office after looking over the MPs' security information one last time.

It was the big day, and I was filled with both excitement and trepidation, and I was also bloody exhausted.

Not that I was complaining. I'd taken *the better than any book boyfriend challenge* very seriously. It had been absolutely fantastic but at the same time, pretty exhausting. However, I'd been determined to pull out all the stops so that by the time we were ready to commit this heist, Melissa knew just how good we could be together. Because when all of this was over, I needed to make sure that she was willing to remain with me and give our relationship a real chance.

I probably shouldn't have gone in for another round

last night though, I thought ruefully, just as I had done every morning since my Little Miss Pouty Lips came to stay. However, like an addict looking for his next fix, I just couldn't resist her and once was never enough. Nevertheless, I really should have got more rest for the day ahead. At least I had let Melissa sleep in for once. She had a tough job ahead and would need all her energy and focus to pull it off without me taxing her.

My body felt sluggish as I pulled myself out of my chair. I needed a cup of coffee, or maybe a bucket full. I yawned, my mouth stretching so wide it was a wonder I didn't swallow the entire room. Fuck, I really was tired!

Rubbing my eyes, I wished I had spent more time in bed last night actually sleeping. Maybe then I wouldn't be worrying about fuelling up on caffeine and adrenaline to stay awake. However, Melissa was too delicious to resist.

Sighing heavily, I headed to the dining room in search of my caffeine fix.

Everyone else was already there, including Melissa. She got up from her seat, approached me, and kissed my cheek.

"I missed you this morning," she said pouting, and my heart soared.

"I wanted to check some stuff before we head off later," I replied willing my cock to stay down.

"You look tired," she stated, her hand brushing across my cheek soothingly.

I grabbed her around the waist and pulled her into me.

"That's because some sexy Little Miss Pouty Lips kept me up all night. Literally," I murmured, grinning at her.

She laughed.

"It wasn't me who wanted to go for round three, Mr Sexy Nerd," she whispered in my ear before slipping out of my arms.

"Sit, the coffee's on the table. I'll get you some breakfast. You need the fuel," she told me.

"Thanks," I said, obeying her.

Warmth spread through me as I watched her head to the buffet area. I liked that she wanted to look after me in this way, it made me feel special. I'd better not tell my brothers that. They ribbed me enough as the youngest boy without telling them how gooey inside I felt whenever Melissa did something nice for me.

Like them, I had a possessive, protective and very dominant streak running through me about a mile wide. So, I tended to prefer taking care of Melissa. However, now and then, I didn't mind her reciprocating. Melissa enjoyed showing she cared as much as I did, and that thrilled me.

My cock was at it again, jerking, as I watched her pout her lips as she decided what to pile on my plate. Exhausted or not, nothing stopped my cock from reacting whenever Melissa was near, or, in fact, whenever I even thought about her.

Melissa smiled as she returned to the table with a plate stacked with eggs, bacon, and toast.

"Got to keep your strength up," she said with a wink.

My cock gave another jerk, and I squirmed. Shaking my head, I did my best to ignore it.

God, the way I could barely control myself around this woman was disconcerting and yet I couldn't find it in me to care. In fact, I loved how out of control I felt around her. Usually, I held on to my control rigidly, but whenever Melissa was near, I felt lighter inside, even when my unruly member throbbed painfully. Considering the workout it had been getting the last few weeks, you would think it would need a rest, but no.

While I knew I would never let the thing distract me enough to put either of us in danger, it was going to be a bloody uncomfortable experience for me later today if I had to deal with a hard-on throughout the entire heist.

Sighing, I poured myself a strong black coffee and tucked into my breakfast because Melissa was right, I needed the energy.

As I ate, I watched her as she nibbled on some toast and chatted with Sonia and Gracie. Sonia whispered something in her ear, and Little Miss Pouty Lips nodded. All three then burst into giggles, shooting glances my way. Melissa turned to me and winked again while the others grinned. I couldn't help but grin in response as I preened, assuming she was confirming how well I was doing in the *better than any book boyfriend* department.

The guys glanced my way and smirked. I might have been the youngest of us all, but I could give them a run for their money any time. The fact they didn't rib me about it showed me just how concerned they were about what lay ahead.

We had a good primary plan for the heist and several contingencies based around every problem we could think might occur. Miki, in his usual thorough way, had ensured we were as prepared as possible. Yet, it was impossible to cover every scenario. Something totally unexpected could easily throw everything into disarray. That thought had my insides churning, not for myself, but for Melissa. I prayed nothing would go wrong.

Sipping on my coffee, I let its fragrant aroma soothe me. I would be glad when today was over and we had the evidence we needed on the bastard MP and finally got him out of our hair. There had been two more attacks on our businesses recently and several on our ally turned uncle, Glowacki's. Between those and the attacks on Melissa, the MP was far too dangerous to allow to run free any longer.

As I took another bite of bacon, I fervently wished we didn't even have to bother with committing this heist at all. Frankly, I would have preferred to simply kill the fucker, but he was a prominent MP, a member of the UK government, so we needed to tread carefully. Killing him might have been what I wanted to do, but it wasn't the best solution for my family. Unfortunately, that meant we had to deal with him in the manner my dad had with the MP's father, and bring him to justice using the full force of the law.

Melissa's laugh penetrated my thoughts, and I smiled as I watched her giggling again with my sister.

Today was going to be dangerous, and Melissa and I would be in the thick of it. I hated that she would be in danger at all, but there was no choice. Her special skill set was needed to do this job. It couldn't be done without her, no matter how much I wished it could be.

Besides, if I were totally honest, she was probably more capable than me when it came to dealing with this sort of thing. If anything went wrong with the heist, it would probably be my sexy little cat burglar that got us through it. If anything threatened her safety, well, that was different; I would deal with that. No matter what happened, we'd get through it together.

After breakfast, Melissa headed off to our room, and I headed back to my office to get started on the first part of the plan.

It took some time at first, but after hacking into the MP's security system a few times, I knew the initial levels wouldn't be a problem. The last two levels, though, would be tougher. That's where Luca and Melissa came in. Their expertise was crucial.

Within three weeks, Luca had worked his usual magic, worming his way into a prime position as one of the MP's top personal guards. The guy was a bloody genius at infiltrating our enemies and one of our best assets.

By planting evidence on one of the MP's closest bodyguards, sparking doubts about his loyalty and subsequently getting him fired, Luca had created an opening for himself. Then he had also orchestrated a disturbance at a rally, leading to an attack on the MP by the crowd. Luca swooped in to save the MP's life, earning his trust in the process. His position had allowed him to obtain the MP's fingerprints and the other detailed information I needed to navigate my way through all but the last level of security. I'd need to bypass that when we were inside.

Once I'd done all I could to prepare, I packed my laptop and other gadgets I'd need into a small backpack. Then double checked everything just to be sure.

Now, it was just a matter of waiting. With an hour still to go, I set an alarm on my phone and leaned back in my chair for a quick nap.

CHAPTER 23
MELISSA
SAME DAY – BRING IT ON!

After breakfast, I left Marko and headed up to our room for some stretching and yoga. I then spent the next couple of hours running through the gymnastic moves I'd need later.

Though it had been a while since I used these skills on a job, daily yoga kept me fit, and years of gymnastics made the moves second nature. Traversing a laser beam assault course, however, was the real challenge.

I'm slim, but my big boobs made squeezing through tight spaces a challenge. Each tight space was awkwardly positioned between laser beams that could burn me and trigger alarms. The skin-tight suit I wore helped by flattening my chest a bit, but extreme caution was still necessary. So, I practiced relentlessly all morning.

Afterwards, I grabbed a glass of milk from the kitchen to help settle my stomach and curled up on the bed with my laptop.

Nervousness gnawed at me. I couldn't remember being this anxious. Working with Dad in the past, I always felt confident. My role had been supportive, and I relied on his expertise to get us through. This time, I was the lead, with Marko as my support. That shift made me nervous. Not because I doubted Marko—I trusted him completely—but because, for the final layer of the MP's security, I'd be on my own. And it was up to me to secure the information we needed.

The main problem I had with that was remembering the sequence for setting up the gadget Marko gave me to download the MP's hard drive undetected. It wasn't complicated, but I kept getting it muddled. I'd devised an acronym to remember it, and it had worked until this morning. Now, my mind kept blanking.

I'd been staring at it for over an hour, repeating the acronym and its meaning in my head. One moment I was sure I had it, the next it was a complete blank.

Finally, I gave in and wrote the acronym on the inside of my wrist. That should help. Now, I just had to remember what it stood for. I glanced at it again, relieved it hadn't rubbed off.

God, I needed to get a grip. I had to stay calm and trust that when the time came, I'd thrive under pressure as usual, not crumble as I feared.

I didn't want to get through all this only to fail at the crucial moment. We'd be pressed for time inside the secret office, and if I couldn't remember what to do, we'd be doomed.

Nothing could go wrong. The thought of failing Marko and his family was unbearable. They'd been so good to me, welcoming me into their fold over the last three weeks. I didn't want to let myself down, but even more, I didn't want to let them down. They had put their trust in me, and I had to prove myself worthy.

Despair washed over me, and I clenched my fists, taking a deep breath to keep from screaming. Closing my eyes, I took another deep breath, and willed myself to relax. I imagined the warmth of my dad's reassuring hug, just like he always gave before a job, and felt a sense of calm.

It was going to be okay. I was overthinking and worrying for nothing. Marko had the hacking skills, I had the burglary skills, and Miki was a brilliant strategist. With the rest of the team, we'd pull this off. I hoped. Fingers crossed! Everything crossed!

I opened my eyes just as Marko pulled me into a tight embrace. His arms around me were comforting and his presence reassured me that everything was going to be okay.

"It's time. Are you ready?" he asked.

"Bring it on!" I said, my nerves replaced with a surge of excitement.

CHAPTER 24
MARKO
STILL THE SAME DAY – WAITING!

Huddled behind the false back of one of Marcie's refrigerated food trucks, sitting facing Melissa with our knees tucked up and toes touching, wasn't the most comfortable way to travel. The journey to the MP's country estate seemed endless, and I was desperate to finally stretch my legs.

By the time we got there, I was so bloody stiff I thought that my legs might snap as soon as I stood up. This sitting quietly doing nothing while we waited for the event to start and the coast to be clear, so we could slip out of the van and begin our mission, was making me anxious. The longer we waited, the more anxious I got. My stomach was doing a very good impression of a rollercoaster right now and I wished I hadn't eaten quite so much at breakfast. I'd been in plenty of perilous situations in the past and wasn't afraid for me, but I was terrified of anything going wrong and something happening to Melissa.

It amazed me how quickly my sexy little cat burglar had become so important to me that all I could think about was her. Sometimes my preoccupation with her almost bordered on obsession. No matter what I was doing, she was never far from my thoughts even to the point that I no longer spent every waking minute, and often most sleeping ones, in front of a computer. Still, I guessed that wasn't such a bad thing as my life had been very insular lately, focused solely on bringing down enemies and keeping my family safe.

However, now that Melissa had come into it, I found myself making plans for a future I hadn't even considered before. I'd always fancied travelling and while we were certainly rich enough for me to do that, I had never actually pursued that dream because frankly there had never been the time when I wasn't needed at home. Now, however, I could see myself taking a long trip with Melissa when all of this was over and we stopped the MP. After all, if our world was finally free of enemies, then I could easily take a break at last and let my team deal with the day to day running of things.

The idea became more appealing as I sat there wiggling my toes in an effort to put feeling back into my legs. Of course, I had to get Melissa onboard with that and we'd have to wait until she'd finished her college course, but I was definitely going to broach the subject with her.

"Provided she'll stay with you after all this is over." The annoying voice in my head said, reminding me that her doing so wasn't yet a done deal.

Pursing my lips, I glanced at Melissa. Her eyes were closed, lips pouting in that irresistible way. God, I loved those pouty lips. I longed to pull her into my arms and kiss her; it would've been a perfect way to pass the time. But I restrained myself. We couldn't afford distractions. We needed to stay focused and silent; discovery wasn't an option. And anyway, it would have been bloody awkward in this tight space, but I was longing to get this operation over with so I could get my woman back home and preferably into my bed.

My eyes caressed her face lovingly and my cock stirred to attention despite my whole bottom half being otherwise numb from lack of movement. Melissa really was a beauty. I couldn't help but smile as I looked at her. My sexy little cat burglar was exceptional in every way. Not only gorgeous, with a great body—which I'd explored thoroughly over the past weeks—but she also had a sharp mind, possibly even sharper than mine. And she was brave enough to tackle what needed to be done today.

Beauty, bravery, and brains. I loved her!

Wow! The words hit me with the force of an articulated lorry at full speed, knocking the breath from my lungs. I hadn't said the words to her yet, I hadn't even admitted them to myself, but I knew them to be true with all my heart.

Under other circumstances, falling in love with someone after just three weeks might be considered unbelievable, but with everything we'd shared in that short time, it just seemed inevitable that love would blossom between us.

Although I had to admit, I had been half in love with Melissa since I first saw her photograph, and even then I knew it wouldn't take me long to fall completely under her spell. In fact, if I was being honest with myself it only took me a couple of days, and the rest of the time we had spent together just solidified my feelings. The last three weeks had been filled with passion and excitement as I got to know my Little Miss Pouty Lips better. And oh, how I got to know her. Every inch of her!

And with that thought, my cock was rock hard, straining against my trousers, making my position even more uncomfortable. Geez, I needed to stop letting my thoughts drift to anything other than the task ahead.

To distract myself, I mentally reviewed our plan.

Time was of the essence, but after all the practise I had done, I knew I could easily pass through the first levels of the MP's security quickly. It was the final two levels that were time consuming, because it would take time for Melissa to make her way safely through that bloody assault course of laser beams in the vault. While she did that, I had to hack the code to open the door of his secret office. Hacking that code would take the longest for me because he changed it weekly, and none of his bodyguards ever entered his secret office; so only he knew the code.

Assuming we had no issue with that, Melissa would then enter his office, attach the small gadget I'd given her, which would let me download the hard drive from his computer, and take a quick look around for other evidence while that happened. And she had to do that and be back out within five minutes. My nerves were fraught, and I prayed there would be no issues.

Worry gnawed at me as I glanced at Melissa again. Her eyes were still closed, her breathing slow and steady. She wasn't sleeping, likely meditating to stay calm and focused. I wished I could do the same.

When this was all over and there was no more danger, I planned on telling Little Miss Pouty Lips how I felt. I believed she felt the same way about me and would agree to stay with me. It would be the culmination of what had been an intense and mind-blowing three weeks. At least I bloody hoped so. I didn't know how I'd deal with it if she didn't.

The very thought of her not wanting me permanently, like I did her, made me feel sick and my stomach churned again. I took several long, slow, steadying breaths to calm myself. That wouldn't happen. I'd worked bloody hard to win her over, and I was pretty sure our feelings matched. Soon, we'd discuss things and clear up any lingering doubts between us, and then we could plan our future together. That thought calmed my nerves, and I glanced at my watch. Not long now.

Opening my laptop, I quickly hacked into the security cameras of the MP's home and recorded clips to use in a loop later to cover us while we were inside. Then I sent a quick message to Miki to let him know the second stage of the plan was done and waited his response. As soon as

Luca was in position, Miki would let us know and we would get out of this bloody claustrophobic space finally.

A few minutes later, Miki's response arrived. Finally!

"Show time," I whispered to Melissa, and her eyes flicked open.

We both stifled groans as we slowly pulled ourselves up to stand and shifted from side to side to bring feeling back into our bodies.

When I felt more capable of movement, I pulled her into me and gave her a quick peck on the lips.

"Ready?" I asked, keeping my voice low.

She nodded and smiled, but I could see the nervousness behind it.

"It's going to be okay. We can do this together," I whispered, instilling as much confidence into the words as I could, not only for her sake, but for my own.

Slowly and as quietly as possible, I slid open the panel, concealing the secret compartment we'd been hiding in.

The door was pulled down, leaving just a few inches gap at the bottom, as expected. I pushed a small camera on a moveable arm under the gap and checked around the outside of the vehicle. All was clear. I nodded for Melissa to come forward with our bags.

Silently, we donned our backpacks, slipped out of the catering truck, and headed to the staff entrance.

CHAPTER 25
MELISSA
STILL THE SAME DAY - THE HEIST!

Taking cover behind a large rubbish bin near the staff entrance, I could hear music and laughter from the party not far away. I waited as Marko disabled the security camera above us, then we crept out and rapped lightly on the door.

As planned, within seconds, Luca opened it, and we dived inside. Marko fiddled with his tablet again, hacking into the main security system to start a pre-recorded loop of the security feed he had recorded while we waited in the truck. This way, we could do what we had to without anyone in the guard room being the wiser. Or so we hoped.

Luca left us to return to his post as bodyguard to the MP before he was missed. Almost all the MP's staff and his twenty-strong security team were at the party, but a few guards remained in the security office at the gate. Even for an MP, his security seemed over the top. Paranoid much? Given his dual life—legitimate MP by day, criminal by night—I supposed he had plenty of enemies and reason for such protection.

We headed along the short hallway and down the stairs towards the basement. Everything was running to plan; fingers crossed it stayed that way. As soon as I had that thought, I hoped I hadn't jinxed us.

While we sneaked inside, Marcie was ensuring the MP was distracted at the party. I just hoped she could do that without him becoming suspicious of her actions. If he did, she could be in real trouble. Who knew what he might do? I shuddered at the thought and sent a silent prayer to my dad in heaven to watch over us all. I was nervous. Marko's hacking skills were phenomenal, so I had no concern there. But I was worried about my own role.

The part which worried me the most was still obtaining the information we came here for, but navigating the laser beams felt just as scary now, as my body was still so stiff from remaining stuck in the one position for so long. God, I wished we'd found a way around that bloody retinal scanner which operated that part of the security system.

My dad had once explained retinal scanners to me. Apparently, they detected unique patterns on a person's retinal blood vessels using low-energy infrared light, converting the data into a computer code. Capillaries absorbed more of the infrared light than surrounding tissues, and the difference in how much light was reflected was measured and assigned numbers, which are then turned into a computer code and the authorised code allowed access to unlock whatever the scanner is locking.

So, unfortunately, short of cutting the MP's eyes out, which was a definite no-no unless we wanted to kill him, there was only one other way through it, with me tackling laser beams like an assault course. Although I wasn't in danger of losing a toe or something, I could get a nasty burn, and any wrong move would trigger the alarm system and get us caught, which could prove fatal to us. My hands shook at the thought.

Considering where we were trying to break into, and the information that was hidden, there was no way the MP would simply alert the authorities and turn us over to them. He wouldn't want to risk that. Besides, once he unmasked us, he would realise immediately who Marko and I were, and likely have his men execute us then and there, before Miki could even think about launching one of his rescue plans.

My heart raced as we moved silently through the hall and downstairs to the basement and towards the MP's offices. The weight of the mission pressed heavily on my shoulders. The thought of what could go wrong looped endlessly in my mind, and I struggled to steady my breathing. I wiped my sweaty palms on my pants, feeling the pressure of the situation tightening my chest. As I waited for Marko to do his thing, I slipped on the glove my Mr Sexy Nerd had created, with the MP's thumbprint that Luca had obtained for us, and concentrated on my breathing.

Once Marko finished what he was doing, he nodded, and I pressed my thumb to the scanner and entered the code Mathieson gave us. My hands shook. The code was incorrect! Damn, I messed up!

"It's okay, calm down, sweetheart," Marko whispered.

Taking a deep breath, I tried again, but my hands were still shaking. I hit the same number twice.

Shit! Shit! Shit! We only had three tries before the alarm would go off. I had just wasted two!

For fuck' sake! I needed to get myself under control, or I was definitely going to set off the alarm. All I had to do was key in a short code. It shouldn't be this hard.

I gulped. My overactive imagination was currently playing me the theme tune for Jaws in my head as if to emphasise the danger. Geez, I needed to get a grip. Fast!

You can do it! You got this! I chanted inside my head to drown out the shark attack music. My breathing was ragged as I felt my panic rise. Focus! I chided myself. If I fucked this up, we could end up dead.

"Look at me, Melissa," Marko said. My eyes flew to meet his.

"Honey, breathe, you've got this. I believe in you," he said, smiling.

Marko believed in me. And just like that, I felt better. Calmer! My breathing slowed and my heart stopped trying to beat its way out of my chest. Marko had faith in me, the way I had faith in him. Neither of us would let the other down.

My confidence restored, I turned back to that bloody keypad and re-entered the code. Relief filled me as the door clicked open.

We made our way into the MP's office. It looked like an ordinary office, but we knew of the secret panel within which hid the next doorway, behind which was my next hurdle before we got to the final secret room where all the information on the MP's illicit operations was stored.

After sliding the panel aside, I entered the one code Mathieson had given me in his letter. Thankfully, this one was still the same, and the door clicked open. Yes!

Marko took a position in a corner, staying out of my way but keeping a close watch. While he set up his systems to crack the final security code, I activated the haze machine we'd brought. It wouldn't reveal the beams as solid lines like in the movies, but it would make their positions visible. The rest was up to me.

I took a moment to survey the room. Relief coursed through me. The pattern of the beams wasn't as complex as I had feared; they resembled the one I had tackled before. That boosted my confidence. Taking a few seconds, I rolled my neck to loosen up and stretched out my arms and legs, finally shaking off the prior stiffness.

When I was ready, I carefully stepped over the first beam. It was mid-thigh height, so I cleared it with ease.

The next beam was much lower, with several others criss-crossing above. The only way past them was to crawl underneath.

Slowly, I lowered myself into the side splits, then bent forward until my chest hit the floor. Stretching my arms under the beam, I used them for leverage, dragging my body forward until I cleared it.

Relaxation set in as I began to enjoy the challenge. I always enjoyed gymnastics, and navigating these beams was a thrilling test of skill. How fun would it be to play with this sort of course without the element of danger? Maybe I could convince Marko to help me set up something similar at home?

Home! Yes, Marko and the Rominov residence had quickly become a place of happiness and peace for me. I loved the house and the people in it and I especially loved the sexy nerd who I knew would be watching my every move right now with lust in his eyes and likely an uncomfortable presence making itself known in his pants.

My heart warmed at the thought of my Russian Bratva man. As soon as everything with the MP was over and he was safely out of the way, I was going to Mr Sexy Merd how I felt. I wanted to stay with him after all of this was over and see where the future took us.

"First, you need to get through the rest of this mission," I reminded myself, snapping my focus back to what I was doing.

Pulling myself into a sitting position, I transitioned to a normal split and carefully brought my legs together. Standing up in the tight space was tricky, but I managed it. Thank goodness I was so flexible.

The next challenge involved horizontal beams spaced less than a foot apart. Turning sideways, I held my breath, bent forward, and flattened my back. Balancing on my right leg, I bent my left knee and slowly extended it to pass through the second and third beams.

Shuffling my right foot closer, I held the position, then slowly lowered my left leg. When my toes touched the ground, rising onto the toes of my right foot, I sucked in my stomach, said a quick prayer, and carefully manoeuvred my hips through the gap. The process felt agonisingly slow, but within a few seconds, I was clear. Pulling my right leg through, I stood up and let out a relieved breath!

The movement left me standing side-on in the perfect position to pass through the next set of beams, which were vertically positioned. I was over halfway to the end, so I took the time to allow myself a few more deep breaths to keep calm.

Even though they were slightly closer together, I sidestepped through them quickly, glad that the all-in-one I had on flattened my boobs and lifted my bum.

Three more sets of beams lay ahead. The first was another horizontal set, identical to the previous one, so I tackled it in the same way. Next came a set similar to the first, and I slipped into side splits, repeating my initial moves. Having tackled these before boosted my confidence, allowing me to navigate them more swiftly this time.

Finally, I came to the last but trickiest set of beams and my nerves kicked in again. This was going to be tough.

My hands shook, and my stomach churned. Sucking in a breath, I held it before slowly releasing it again. I needed to gain control; even a millimetre off could spell disaster.

Closing my eyes, I heard my dad's voice giving me one of his pep talks.

"Come on, Melissa. This is child's play. Focus and discipline are all you need."

Feeling more positive, I breathed deeply, forcing myself to relax as I took a few seconds to think through my next moves.

Eyes narrowed; I studied the beams. Several horizontal beams ran along the bottom, reaching hip height, but they were too close to pass through. Above them, criss-crossed beams formed a web; the only way through was to shimmy between them at their widest point.

Visualising the best path, I took another deep breath to steady my nerves and moved forward an inch. There was no time for second-guessing. Bending at the waist, I placed my hands flat on the ground. With my weight on them, I carefully lifted my legs, straightening into a handstand, and shuffled closer to the beams.

Slowly and deliberately, I lowered my legs behind me, threading them between the criss-crossed beams until my feet touched the ground. In a back bend, I shuffled the tiniest bit forward, keeping my back high to avoid touching the beams. Transferring all my weight to my feet, I tightened my core and slowly, inch by inch I lifted my torso up and shimmied my body through the lasers in a limbo style movement. When my head cleared them, I stood and turned towards Marko. I felt like jumping for joy, but I restrained myself and settled for a grin and a wink.

CHAPTER 26
MARKO
STILL THE SAME DAY - THE ESCAPE!

As Melissa contorted her body into awe-inspiring positions, my mouth hung open. Knowing she could do this stuff and actually seeing her do it were two different things. I was completely mesmerised by every move she made.

The breath caught in my throat as I watched her tackle the final beams, shimmying beneath them with meticulous precision. When she turned toward me, smiling after completing the most impressive feat of agility I'd ever witnessed, I exhaled in a rush.

My sexy little cat burglar was practically buzzing with the energy radiating from her, and the joy on her face made my heart race. A wave of desire surged through me, threatening to bring me to my knees. God, that was nerve-wracking and the sexiest thing I'd ever seen.

I'd assumed that her years of gymnastics had made her flexible, but I hadn't quite realised just how flexible.

Seeing her complete those moves made all kinds of wicked thoughts race through my mind.

I wonder if I can get her to do that in sexy lingerie later? Or better yet naked?

Melissa's display left me hornier than any lap dance I'd ever experienced. I definitely planned to explore those moves on a more intimate level in the future. My mind swirled with images of things I hoped to try, and I zoned out lost in my fantasies as a grin spread across my face and I adjusted myself.

"Your turn!" she said, snapping me out of my daydreams.

Huh? What? Oh, right! Yes! Work! Dangerous situation! Need to move! My addled brain finally came back online. Geez! I needed to get a grip.

Forcing my thoughts back to the task at hand, I glanced at the tablet and was happy to see that the two codes were in front of me.

"Ready, honey?" I asked, and she nodded and turned towards the key panel as I called out the numbers of the first code.

My stomach churned as I watched with bated breath. There were three red lights, but almost immediately after she typed the code in, one turned green, then the other amber, and the final one remained red but started flashing.

"Sweetheart, calm down. The worst part is over. All we need to do now is input four numbers. Then you do exactly what we rehearsed, and the next park with be easy, compared to what you've just done. You're exceptional, Melissa, and you've got this," I said.

After a deep breath, she tried the numbers again, gasping in relief as all the lights turned green. The beams shut off, and the door clicked open with one second to spare. Fuck, that was cutting it fine.

"Five minutes starting now," I said, and she darted into the room with a quick nod. Heart pounding, hands sweating, I prayed nothing would go wrong. This was the most vital part of our plan, and Melissa had just five minutes to execute it and return before the system reset and the beams reactivated. Failure meant serious trouble.

Ideally, both of us would have accessed the room, but traversing those beams was beyond my skill set, so I had to settle for waiting. Still, my faith in my little cat burglar's abilities reassured me; I knew she'd get the job done. Despite my belief in her, the wait was torturous. Every second dragged on.

We had estimated the device I gave her would need about two minutes to hack into the MP's system. My invention, a compact but powerful handheld device equipped with top-tier hacking software, was designed to complete the task swiftly. It would then take an additional couple of minutes to transfer the data to my computer back at the Estate.

While it did that, Melissa would be looking through the rest of the room, taking photos of everything else she could find to do with the MP's illegal activities. We couldn't steal the information, as we needed it to be found by the authorities at a later date, but we could copy it. And we needed to get enough evidence for our contacts in Interpol to get a warrant to search the property and investigate the MP.

That's why we had to be as stealthy as possible and gather the evidence we needed while leaving no trace of actually being here. All going well, we'd be in and out and the MP would never know we'd been. That way, he wouldn't move or destroy the evidence before the authorities could be alerted.

Checking my watch, I saw four and a half minutes had already passed. My heart threatened to burst out of my chest, it was pounding so hard. Melissa was cutting it close. With the security system about to reactivate in under 30 seconds and guards set to patrol the grounds again soon, we had to get out quickly to avoid capture.

Finally, she emerged, closing the door with ten seconds to spare. The beams stayed off as she sprinted back across the room. A quick hug was all I managed before the beams flickered back on. We grabbed our equipment and retraced our steps, as I reset the various security layers as we went.

At the exit, Melissa pushed open the door and scanned the area for safety before stepping out. The moment we were outside, I reset the security cameras to the live feed, giving us mere seconds to escape before the system kicked in.

Melissa grabbed my hand, and we dashed to the catering van just as two security guards rounded the corner. Spotting us in our all-black outfits, they shouted for us to stop.

Shit! Our original escape plan had been to hide back inside the catering truck and wait there until the event was over and Marcie drove it away. That was no longer possible.

Instead, we jumped into the front of the truck. Grabbing the set of spare keys Marcie had deliberately left inside, I stated the engine, and sped off before the guards could reach us.

Gunning it down the long driveway, I checked my side mirror in time to see a guard shouting into his radio, likely alerting the gate to our approach. Damn!

Another couple of guards stood in front of the closed gate, waving at us to stop. No chance!

"Hold on, I'm going to ram it!" I shouted, putting my foot down and pushing the van to its limit.

Fortunately, the guards decided against playing chicken with us and leapt out of the way. One guard fired at the van, but we were moving too fast; his shots mostly missed, grazing the side of the vehicle only once before we barrelled through and sped away.

Melissa screamed as we slammed into the gate, ripping it from its hinges. Thank god we'd reinforced the front of Marcie's van when we adapted it to include the hidden compartment.

Relief washed over me as we cleared the MP's property, but it was short-lived.

"Shit, we're being pursued!" Melissa yelled.

Through the wing mirror, I saw one black SUV emerge from the driveway, followed by another. Hell, how did they catch up so fast?

As I floored it, I told Melissa to contact Miki. Escape plan A was a bust, so Escape Plan B was underway.

Up ahead, a tractor pulled out behind us, blocking the road. Driven by one of our guys in farmer's attire, it crawled slowly, forcing the SUVs to slow down. I sniggered; that should hold them. Unfortunately, it didn't. Soon, the SUVs were swerving around the tractor, cutting through hedging into a field, and then back onto the road.

Damn it! It was time to up the ante. Flooring the van, I tried to distance us from the SUVs, but losing them on these country roads wasn't going to be easy.

"Any chance we can actually shake them?" Melissa asked, glancing back nervously.

"Not here," I said, tightening my grip on the steering wheel. "We need a diversion."

Melissa radioed Miki again, her voice tense. "Miki, it's time for another diversion. We're heading to the next point now."

"Got it. Trigger is ready," Miki's voice crackled back. "Stay safe."

"Here we go," Melissa said, eyes widening.

As expected, Trigger was waiting up ahead with an actual farmer at the side of the road. I sped past them, and in the rearview mirror, I saw Trigger open the gate in the fence.

Next thing we knew, sheep were heading onto the road, creating another roadblock.

"With luck, that should slow them down this time," I said with a grin, watching the SUVs struggle to manoeuvre through the large flock.

Unfortunately, luck wasn't on our side and the bloody sheep moved too fast. Instead of blocking the way for a good few minutes, as we had hoped, the stupid creatures hurried off the road into the lay-by. Despite the best efforts of Trigger and the farmer we'd bribed, the road was empty again within a few seconds, and the first SUV pushed on past them to continue its pursuit of us. The other one only took a few more seconds to follow.

Damn, damn, and damn again! Plan B was to halt or slow down any pursuit to allow us to get clear of the country roads and make it to the motorway where we could speed off and get away easier. It was not working.

CHAPTER 27
MELISSA

MELISSA (STILL THE SAME DAY – ONTO PLAN C!

The van careened around another sharp bend, the tires squealing as Marko gripped the wheel with white-knuckled determination. I glanced in the side mirror and saw the two SUVs still hot on our trail. My heart pounded in my chest, a wild rhythm that echoed the chaos outside.

"Can't you go any faster?" I shouted over the roar of the engine, my voice trembling with a mix of fear and adrenaline.

Marko's jaw was set, his eyes fixed on the road ahead.

"I'm trying, Melissa!" he snapped back, the tension in his voice mirroring my own.

I gripped the edge of my seat as I scanned the road ahead, looking for alternative escape routes, every bump and jolt making me more acutely aware of the thin line we were riding between safety and disaster.

There was nothing for it. We needed to move to plan C.

My voice was shaky, but determined as I radioed Miki again. "Miki, Plan B hasn't worked, it's time to get serious. We need to move to plan C."

"On it," he replied, his tone clipped. "Take the next left and head through the village. There's a rendezvous point a few minutes away."

Miki fired off more instructions about what to do next as Marko followed his directions, winding through the narrow country roads until we reached the edge of the village. We ducked down a side street, where two of Miki's guys stood waiting in overalls. With seconds to spare, they swiftly peeled off the catering signs and customised plates, turning it into a generic white van.

Marko nodded at me, his face tense. "Time to switch rides."

We ripped off our balaclavas and jumped out. Marko quickly slapped a helmet on my head before donning his own. Climbing onto the waiting motorbike, he gestured for me to get on behind him.

The guys eased the van back onto the road just as the two SUVs roared into the village. Although the van's appearance had changed, it still looked the same from behind and the SUVs kept tailing it.

Yes, it was working. Relief poured through me as we watched the vehicles pass us by. Miki's guys were a good distance ahead of the SUV's now and so hopefully by the time the MP's security caught up, and saw there were no catering signs and two different people inside, they'd realise they had been duped and give up.

A few minutes later, Marko pulled out and headed in the same direction. There was no other way out of the village, except the way we'd come and that was not an option as we needed to get out of the area fast.

However, once we were through the village, the plan was to let the van go ahead onto the motorway and lead the SUVs away, then for us to continue along the country road which ran parallel to the motorway for several miles. Once we saw the SUV's end their pursuit, we were to join the motorway at the next junction and head home.

However, yet again, luck was not playing nice, and we rounded a bend to discover a set of temporary traffic lights and unexpected roadworks up ahead had caused the traffic to stop and a long queue to form. Our guys were near the front and the SUV's near the back with just a few cars between us and them.

Oh hell!

My heart pounded as I watched a guy get out of one of the SUV's and run to the front of the van. As realisation dawned that it wasn't their target, the guy rushed back to the vehicles, screaming something into his walkie talkie. He stopped and scanned the road around him, his eyes taking in our bike and I knew without a doubt that he had somehow recognised us

A few seconds later, both vehicles made a U turn and headed back our way.

Panic surged through me. "Marko, they're coming!" I screamed.

"I see them, honey. Hold tight," he replied before

driving up the narrow lay-by and past the line of traffic. Several shots rang out just missing us. Thankfully, our position made it difficult to get a clear shot.

I couldn't believe that despite being on a motorbike instead of in a van, somehow we had been recognised. Probably it was the outfits and backpacks. We had been supposed to turn our jackets inside out to chance their look, but in the excitement, we'd forgotten. Miki was going to have something to say about that later I was sure.

Marko gunned the bike through the lights just as they were turning green and sped past the vehicles in front. Angry horns blasted at us, but they were the least of our concerns.

I held on tight as we sped along a long stretch of road heading towards another slip road for the motorway, praying we could make it there before the SUVs caught up and started firing again.

More horns blasted, and I checked over my shoulder, gasping as I saw the two SUVs quickly gaining on us as they overtook the vehicles behind.

Tearing along the country lanes, my heart pounded, sweat ran down my back, making my top cling to me. My arms ached from my death grip on Marko's waist. It was a wonder he could breathe; I was clinging to him like a limpet, scared I might fall off at any minute.

I might have actually enjoyed the thrill of riding at top speed on the back of a bike with Marko if we weren't being chased and I hadn't been so bloody terrified. Right now, all I could think of was getting off the thing as soon as possible, and preferably in one piece.

I heard Marko radioing Miki through his helmet again, and I guessed Miki must have been getting frantic as Marko gave a sarky reply.

"Nah, thought I'd add some danger into the mix! Spice things up a bit!" he drawled sarcastically.

I could almost see Miki bristle with annoyance at that. I would smile if the situation wasn't so dangerous.

My nerves were fraught, and I kept checking over my shoulder horrified that the MP's men were gaining on us.

"Marko! They're getting closer!" I screamed.

More shots rang out and Marko swerved, weaving along the road in an attempt to keep us from being hit.

Thank God we had Escape Plan D and several others if needed. I was thorough when planning a heist and escape, but Miki was even more so. Although I initially thought the number of scenarios he planned for was overkill, I was now glad he did. I couldn't get off this bike fast enough.

A minute later, we pulled onto the next slip road to the motorway with the SUVs in hot pursuit. Holding on as if my life depended on it, which it did, I screamed as Marko weaved in and out of traffic, changing lanes to stop them from gaining on us.

Suddenly Marko, shot between two lorries as one overtook the other before crossing multiple lanes onto another bit of motorway.

Fuck! Shit! Geez! We barely missed being pulverised by a lorry.

Marko's laughter rang out, and I realised he was actually bloody enjoying this.

"I'm never getting on a bike with you again!" I screamed.

The madman just laughed harder.

"Oh, come on, honey. If we weren't being shot at, you know you would love this," he said, his body vibrating with amusement.

When I thought about it, he was probably right, but I wasn't going to tell him that. The guy didn't need any further encouragement to do more crazy shit right now.

"Psycho!" I shouted, biting back a chuckle before it could betray me.

One of the SUVs gained on us, and the passenger fired a shot. They were much closer now, and the next shot grazed my helmet. Fuck sake! That was way too close for comfort. I almost peed my pants.

We swerved across lanes again, just managing to avoid more shots. We had almost passed the next junction, but just as the SUV pulled into the lane beside us, Marko tugged us sharply to the left and onto the slip road and off the motorway.

The SUV beside us couldn't follow. The security guard in the passenger seat, who had been shooting, shouted and cursed as we whizzed by out of firing range. Thank God for that!

But we weren't in the clear yet. The other SUV which had fallen behind was now headed onto the slip road in pursuit of us.

"The other one's still on our tail," I shouted to Marko.

"Don't worry, we'll lose them in the tunnel," he replied, before barking off instructions to Miki.

We headed along an expressway and headed towards a tunnel up ahead. As we approached a large lorry, Miki slowed to match the vehicle's speed, and I watched in amazement as the back opened, descending to form a ramp. Geez, this was like something out of Mission Impossible or the Fast and Furious movies.

Lights came on inside as Marko drove the bike straight up and onto a bike rack, stopping and clipping it in place as the makeshift ramp closed behind us.

Romi was driving the lorry and called our helmets to check if we were okay. Thankfully, he confirmed that, as expected, we'd lost the SUV in the tunnel and we were finally heading home to the Estate.

"Thank fuck for that!" I cried in relief, jumping off the bike as soon as I could and removing my helmet.

That was a close call. Either of us could have been hurt, or worse. I was shaking with adrenaline, the fear of the last few hours turning to elation at having finally got away.

Despite having just pried myself off him, I was suddenly gripped with an overwhelming need to be close to Marko again.

Mr Sexy Nerd obviously felt the same as he grabbed me, kissing me like he couldn't get enough, grabbing my ass and grinding his erection against me. He was frantic, and so was I.

Wild with need, he pulled down the zip of my jumpsuit, reaching inside to squeeze my breasts before taking my mouth again. The kiss deepened, and I fought back a moan. Marko's touch was electric. It felt like I was burning up for him, every part of me on fire. I always felt a burning need for Marko, but this was beyond that.

Nearly losing someone you care about always heightened your emotions, but when it happened in a dangerous situation with adrenaline pumping, it obviously heightened them even more until you needed reassurance, confirmation that you were both alive. This frantic need was that for us. I needed to touch him as much as he did me, to know we survived.

Panting hard, we broke apart, still touching, not wanting to lose contact. Marko lifted my leg, and pulled off my boot, then did the same with the other, tossing them aside. Pushing my jumpsuit off my shoulders, he quickly stripped me of that, kissing and touching each part of my body as he exposed me to him.

When I stood completely naked before him, I turned the tables on my sexy Russian and pulled his clothing off.

As soon as I'd divested him of his boxers, Marko grabbed me, turning me so my back was pressed to his front. Squeezing my breasts from behind, his fingers kneaded the flesh, moulding them in his palms while he nibbled my neck. His hands and hot breath on my body drove me insane until I felt feverishly desperate for him.

Holding me close, his erection pressing against my lower back, he pinched my nipples as he walked me toward the bike. My thighs were slick with my juices, and my pussy pulsed with need.

"Mount!" he commanded. That sexy Russian accent came out in full force, and I shivered and quickly obeyed.

If any other man ordered me around during intimacy, I would have told him where to go, but with Marko, I loved it. As long as he only did it during sex, I could handle that. I was far too independent to allow him to dominate me outside of the bedroom. But inside, well, my sexy Russian could bring it on!

Marko climbed on behind me still holding me tightly against him as if he couldn't bear to let me go even a little.

"Grab the handles!" he commanded again, pushing me forward.

When I did what I was told, he lowered his hands to my hips, moving me where he wanted me, and I let him.

It felt so very decadent to be straddling the bike wet and naked like this.

Covering me with his body, Mr Sexy Nerd slipped one hand around to the front of me again to play with my nipples. First one, then the other, while his other hand slipped between my wet folds and his cock ground between my cheeks.

"So wet," he whispered breathlessly, nuzzling my ear, his hands working their magic.

Our movements sped up as we ground our bodies together, and he nipped and licked at my neck. Fisting my ponytail, he pulled my head back, exposing my neck further while he continued to play with my clit. Biting and sucking hard, where my neck and shoulder met, I realised he was marking me. I was going to have a hickey! My eyes widened, and I clamped my teeth into my bottom lip to keep from giggling.

I was a grown woman, not a silly teenager, so I should not be happy about that, but I was. Some primal part of me loved the fact that this gorgeous man wanted me and wanted everyone to know it by marking me as his.

The thought made me even wetter, and I moaned, grinding against his fingers as I neared my release. A sheen of sweat burst out on my skin and I shuddered as it hit me.

Oh my god, that was so good, and he isn't even finished!

Grasping my hips in a punishing grip, Marko lifted them up slightly before thrusting his cock all the way into me.

Marko tugged my ponytail, making my back arch. The slight sting of pain heightening my pleasure. Wow! He hit me so deep in that position.

Murmuring endearments in Russian which made me want to melt into a puddle of goo, my sexy Russian man pounded into me at a punishing pace, tugging on my hair and squeezing my breast as I held on to the bike handles so tightly my knuckles turned white.

Dear god, I was about to come again. I was still in the throes of my second release when he thrust several more times, spilling into me.

My whole body shook with pleasure, and I collapsed forward onto the bike.

"That was bloody amazing, Marko!" I panted through ragged breaths.

The cold metal of the bike was cool against my bare skin, and I grinned wickedly.

"I can never ride a bike again without thinking about this. In fact, I won't even be able to look at one without replaying this in my head," I said, chuckling and trying to catch my breath.

The vibrations of Marko's answering laughter made his cock reawaken inside my body and I groaned as I felt it harden again. Slowly, he started to move, rocking himself against me while I lay sprawled over the bike.

"You're insatiable," I laughed, secretly thrilled by how much this man wanted me.

"I can't deny it," he said, nibbling my ear and building us both up to a frenzy again.

A short while later, we lay there in a heap across the bike once again as we waited for our breathing to even out.

When it eventually did, he climbed off and turned me towards him and took my mouth in a long, lingering kiss.

"God, that was great," he grinned.

"I've always loved riding a bike, but that ride blew me away!" he laughed.

"Can we do it again sometime?" I asked, grinning.

"I thought you were never getting on a bike with me again," he said with a smirk.

"Well, if you can guarantee at least some of the rides

will end up like that, then I'm more than willing to change my mind," I said, nipping his lower lip with my teeth.

"Oh, I will definitely guarantee that," he laughed, tugging my head back to kiss me deeply.

A short while ago, I wasn't sure about getting on a bike with Marko again. However, our sexy escapades had certainly changed my mind, and now I couldn't wait.

CHAPTER 28
MARKO
A WEEK LATER – SHOWER PLAY

It was early morning, and I finished replying to the last email in my inbox and closed my laptop. As always, it had been a long list, but I managed to get through it quickly. I was usually a light sleeper, and it used to be that I would reply to an email the minute I received it, no matter the time, day, or night.

However, since Melissa came into my life, things had changed. Now, I turned my laptop off at night and put my phone on silent, so I could enjoy just being with her. I was glad of the change; I was still as focused on my work, but not as obsessed as I had been.

When my parents were murdered, Miki had to take on the role of Pakhan, and Ash had to be there as his second, while Romi, Luca, and I were needed to back them both up. It had been a difficult time, and while I had all the same skills as the others at fighting, it quickly became apparent that my most prized skill was my gift with computers. With this skill, I could help my family not only in the perilous time with the changeover of Pakhan but also with Miki's vision for a more legitimate future for us. So, I threw myself into my work. In fact, all of us guys had.

Until I met Melissa, this had not really bothered me. Or at least, not much. I had, of course, felt the stirrings of envy when Ash, Romi, Sonia, and Miki all found love, but I hadn't known how much I craved something else in my life, or rather someone. However, the moment I saw Melissa's photograph, I knew she was special, and the moment I met her, I knew I had found a missing piece of me.

So now, my work wasn't everything. Now I had other things to think about, or rather, another person. My Little Miss Pouty Lips was far more important to me than anything else. In such a short time, this woman had changed my life for the better.

As I looked down at Melissa's sleeping form, I couldn't help but smile. Despite only knowing her such a short time, I loved her and could no longer envisage a future without her in it. I had met that one person who fulfilled me. We had a lot in common, both of us grew up in a criminal lifestyle and wanted out. Each of us was highly intelligent and enjoyed thinking outside the box and finding solutions to intricate problems. We had a common enemy and would do whatever it took to stop him. In essence, we were perfect together.

I had been working frantically to decode the MP's hard

drive over the last few days. Last night, I finally managed to. This morning, we were all meeting to view our findings.

"Babe, time to get up!" I whispered in Melissa's ear and she stirred.

Her eyes flew open when I kissed her gently on the forehead.

Grinning wickedly, she reached for me, licking her lips.

"I want to suck that big hard cock!" she smiled with a devilish glint in her eyes as she came up onto her knees eager to take me into her mouth.

"As much as I would love that, I have other plans for you this morning," I said, pulling away.

Some shower action was in my mind as we were short on time and needed to get ready soon.

"Sex while showering will save us a lot of time," I said as I grabbed her off the bed and threw her over my shoulder caveman style.

My sexy cat burglar giggled, and I slapped her bare bum and stalked towards the bathroom.

"Someone's a filthy girl. I'd better wash all that dirt right out of you. Dirty girls need to be punished," I told her in mock severity, doing my best headmaster's voice, as I turned on the shower to warm up the water.

"Yes, sir!" she replied, giggling in agreement.

I thrust her into the large cubicle and followed her in. Turning her to face the wall, I lifted her arms above her head, placing them on the tiles.

"Keep them there!" I commanded while soaping my hands.

The warm water ran down her back, wetting her pert bottom.

"Hmm, gorgeous," I murmured, as I kneaded her cheeks, the slippery feel of her soapy skin making me hard. She moaned and pushed against my palms.

"Stay still!" I commanded, circling my hands around her waist and up to cup her tits.

God, I loved her tits and her bum. In fact, I loved everything about her. Everything she was, everything she did, was a turn on for me and every time with her got better and better. Pinching her nipples, I squeezed them almost bruisingly as I pulled her hard against me.

"Stick your ass out," I demanded, pressing myself against her so she could feel how turned on I was.

The angle pushed her breasts into my hands and her bottom against my crotch in just the right way. Her boobs fit my hands perfectly, and I squeezed them again while I rubbed my erection against her cheeks. Dipping between them ever so slightly. Just enough to tease at her opening.

Melissa gasped and her hands moved from their position as she tried to get closer to me.

Uh uh. Not the plan, sweetheart!

"Hands up or I'll stop!" I slapped her bum hard, and she quickly shoved them back into place, letting out a squeal.

"You have a punishment to take," I told her in my headmaster's voice again.

She turned her head slightly to watch my reaction as she smirked and wiggled against me.

I smacked her again, first on one cheek then the other.

"Oh! Oh!" she cried.

Lust clouded my vision as I looked at the pretty pink colour now staining her beautiful bum. My cock jerked at the sight, and I gulped, sniffing hard to stay in control.

Licking my lips, I reached forward and squeezed those gorgeous breasts again.

"Dirty girls need to be thoroughly cleansed. Don't you agree Miss Martin?" I whispered in her ear, grazing her lobe with my teeth and giving it a slight tug as I tugged each of her nipples.

"Oh, yes, sir," she giggled again, obviously enjoying our role play.

"Do you think this is funny Miss Martin?" I asked, punctuating each word with a hard slap and a stroke of my hand to soothe the sting.

"No, sir!" she cried, her voice catching as my playful antics heightened her desire.

I chuckled.

"Time to cleanse that filthy mind and body of yours," I said with one last spank.

"Don't move those hands. Keep them above your head!" I reminded her.

Grasping her wrists with one hand, I leaned forward and whispered in her ear, "Fuck, you turn me on baby," before I reached between her thighs with the other hand and started stroking her clit.

Melissa groaned, and the sound went straight to my shaft, which throbbed in response. She was soaking wet and not just from the water cascading over her body. Her nub was swollen, and I rubbed it with my soapy fingers while I played with her tits with my other hand. Moving from one to the other, I squeezed and kneaded the flesh, spending extra time on the nipples, pinching then circling them with my thumb and forefingers.

Melissa writhed and moaned, struggling to keep her hands above her head. I loved it. The sounds she made set me on fire. Sweat broke out on my forehead, and I fought to not plunge myself straight into her. I needed her so badly.

Nudging her legs open further with my knee, I kept one hand playing with her luscious boobs and moved the fingers of my other hand towards her entrance. She knew what I had planned and pushed up against my hand, seeking the pleasure my fingers could bring. I was so turned on I couldn't be gentle and plunged three fingers in at once.

Little Miss Pouty Lips cried out as her greedy channel pulled them deeper, milking them with every thrust. She was so close to release, and I couldn't wait to replace my fingers with my cock but first I wanted her to come.

Desperate to make that happen, I pulled her tight against me and increased my rhythm, thrusting hard and deep. She rocked her hips, panting hard and moaning with each thrust.

"That's it, baby. Take them like a good girl, just the

way you'll take my cock," I said, enjoying playing my own role.

Melissa shuddered at my words, and I chuckled to myself I made a mental note to remember to add a bit more role play to our sexy times. After all, I had to keep our sex life interesting since I had so many book boyfriends to outdo.

My eyes closed, and she cried out as her release took hold and her pussy squeezed my cock to the point it was almost painful.

Before she could come down from the high of her orgasm, I immediately removed my fingers and thrust my cock into her. I plunged in fast, then moved out slowly, then back in fast and out slowly, continue this sweet torture as I drew out her orgasm as long as possible. My dirty girl was having none of it though and moved her hands down to find a better purchase on the wall as she tried to thrust back against me.

"Bad girl!" I smacked her bum hard and lifted her hands up again.

"They stay there," I told her as I thrust in and out slowly one more time.

My Little Miss Pouty Lips didn't enjoy being denied, but delayed gratification was always worth the wait, so I continued with my fast, slow rhythm until she was whimpering in need, mumbling incoherently with her cheek pressed against the tiles. My knees were trembling with the effort it took to keep from ramping up the pace, but I wasn't about to end things too soon.

Finally, I took pity on us both, increasing my speed until we were panting and moaning loudly as our release built together and exploded between us.

It was incredible. Every time with her was incredible.

"Well, Miss Martin, I think you have been thoroughly cleansed," I laughed.

"Yes, sir," she giggled back.

As our breathing evened out, I turned her around and kissed her deeply then soaped her all over again and rinsed her off. I quickly cleaned myself and then we got out and despite needing to hurry, spent far too long drying each other off.

As we were getting ready, my phone vibrated. It was Josh.

"I need to get this, sweetheart," I told her, kissing her on the head and heading through to my livingroom.

CHAPTER 29
MELISSA

THE SAME DAY – SEXY AND SILLY AND SICKENED

As I watched Marko's tight bum walking away from me, I licked my lips and bit back a grin. Lord, he had a biteable bum! The man was one gorgeous specimen.

When I woke up this morning, I felt a surge of excitement and a craving to taste him. I'd never been keen on giving blowjobs before, but with Marko, it was different. The way he groaned and moaned, thrusting into my mouth slow and controlled at first but then frantic and desperate, drove me wild. It thrilled me to know I could turn him on like that, that my mouth could bring my dangerous, sexy nerd to such wild abandon. So, when he pulled back, disappointment hit me. But I should have known he had something even better in mind. He always did.

As I got dressed for the day ahead, I felt giddy from our sexy shower play. Who knew being a dirty girl could be so much fun? It almost made me want to go out and roll in the dirt just so Marko would need to take me back to the shower.

Even though I loved my smutty romance books, I never dreamed I'd enjoy role play, let alone having my bottom spanked. But I did love it. Probably because it was Marko doing it. I had to admit, I loved everything that sexy Russian did to me. Everything we did together was so much fun. I couldn't get enough of him, and it wasn't just because of the utterly amazing sex. It was him. Everything about him. Marko was a dangerous male, but he made me feel nothing but safe. In his arms, I felt protected, cared for, respected, and loved.

It might have been early days, but I knew Marko was the one. I couldn't imagine a future without him. In no time, the sexy Russian had become a permanent fixture in my life. Or at least, I hoped he was.

My apartment was being rebuilt, but I no longer wanted to live there. It just wouldn't feel the same. Instead, I planned to rent it out for some extra income. Maybe I'd sell it one day, but I wasn't ready for that yet. When the building was destroyed, I thought the explosion had taken all my memories with it. But I was wrong. The house was gone, but the garden, my mum's favourite place, was still there. Dad and I had planted a rosebush in her memory after she passed, so the place still held some dear memories for me after all.

Since Marko and I hadn't talked about the future, I wasn't sure if I needed to find another place to stay when everything was over. From his hints, I thought he wanted me to remain with him, but since we hadn't discussed it properly, I didn't want to assume. And let's face it, Marko was a domineering guy who knew what he wanted. If he wanted me to stay, wouldn't he just say that?

Frowning, I worried my lip. What if, when the danger was over, he decided we should slow down? Maybe he'd prefer I moved out, got a place of my own, and continued dating him. He might not be ready for more commitment. After all, things had moved fast between us; we started living together the day after we met, and only for my safety.

I knew we both had strong feelings for each other, that was obvious, but did that mean we'd keep living together? What if I felt more for him than he did for me?

Once we dealt with the MP and I was no longer in danger, would his feelings change? Would his interest in me wane? The way he looked at me and treated me made me doubt it, but I could be wrong.

The man himself returned to the bedroom. My eyes followed his every move as he dressed, and my insides lit up when he gave me a sexy smile full of promise.

Grinning, I looked in the mirror to brush my hair and that's when I noticed my reflection. Skin glowing, eyes shining and lips still swollen from Marko's kisses; that was the face of a well-loved woman. I wasn't wrong! My concerns were likely just a product of my usual overthinking. Soon, we'd have that talk and plan our future.

In the meantime, I was determined to enjoy every second with my Mr Sexy Nerd, in bed and out—preferably as much in bed as possible. That thought made me bite my lip to avoid grinning like a madwoman as I watched him finger-comb his hair. Marko gave me another sexy smile, and I blew him a kiss.

The sexy Russian stalked towards me, eyes betraying his naughty thoughts. My heart fluttered, and a surge of dampness rushed to my core. I knew exactly what that look meant. If we didn't get out of this room now, we wouldn't for quite some time and while I really wanted to stay, unfortunately, we had things to do and people to see.

So, I turned, giggling, and ran for the door. I made it to the hallway and glanced back just in time to see his feral grin before he grabbed me. I squealed, the sound catching in my throat as he lifted me and kissed me hard until neither of us could breathe.

"Blowing kisses is for kids. Grown men need a proper kiss," he panted after finally letting us come up for air.

Fisting my hair, my sexy man went in for another kiss as if to prove his point, kissing me until my knees were weak and I was clinging to him unable to stand on my own.

"Now that's how I want you to kiss me every day," he smirked sexily.

"Only if you're a good boy," I said with a grin, darting out of the way as he lunged for me.

"I'm always a good boy," Marko said, catching me from behind before I got more than a couple of steps away.

"In fact, I'm good at a lot of things, and in particular, I'm exceptionally good at being naughty," he said with a chuckle as he captured me in his arms and tickled me mercilessly. I squealed and tried desperately to wriggle out of his grasp. But there was no escape.

Tears of laughter ran down my face, and I could barely speak but managed to gasp out, "Stop! If you don't I'm going to pee my pants!"

Marko burst into fits of laughter but thankfully stopped.

"We can't have that. We don't want you sitting in wet knickers all morning," he chuckled before his eyes turned wicked again, "Or not that kind of wet."

Licking his lips, he reached for me once more, but this time I was faster and took off running. Wicked laughter followed me as he chased me down the hall.

I flew down the stairs, laughing hard and gasping for breath. Marko was right behind me and as we reached the bottom, he caught me again. With one arm wrapped around my body, the other clasped lightly around my throat, he pulled me back against him.

"Chasing you brings out the predator in me, Melissa. It makes me want to do so many things to you," he whispered in a sultry voice that sent shivers down my spine.

As Marko nibbled on my earlobe, I gulped, as a rush of liquid dampened my knickers. Heck, I might not have peed myself, but if he didn't stop now, he would get his way and I'd be sitting squirming in wet panties for the rest of the morning after all. Not to mention, I'd be too bloody horny to think straight. So, for my sanity and hygiene, I needed to dampen his ardour, and fast.

"Did you look through the MP's files when you opened them?" I asked, turning to look at him.

My question had the desired effect. He sniffed and his eyes hardened as he answered. "No, just a quick glance, but that was enough to know we have plenty of evidence to incriminate the bastard!"

Frowning, he led me towards the dining room where we'd arranged to meet the others for breakfast, and I could see the wheels turning in his head. Despite the fact he had said he'd only had a quick glance; I could tell that whatever he'd seen had disturbed him, and I braced myself for what was to come.

"After breakfast, we need to look through the MPs records, decide what we're going to send to the law, then get it to the contact in Interpol we used before," he told me, and I nodded.

It would be good to get this over with, but I was really not looking forward to viewing this stuff.

Everyone must have felt the same, because breakfast was a more solemn affair than usual.

Once it was over, we filed out, saying goodbye to the other women, all of whom had decided not to view the information with us. I didn't blame them, and if it wasn't something I needed to be a part of, I would have opted out, too. From the looks on their faces, I thought most of the guys would have as well, if that had been an option.

Unfortunately, it wasn't, so we piled into Miki's large office along with Janusz Glowacki and his oldest sons. We had met the other day, and I instantly took a liking to all of them.

Janusz Glowacki was the type of good-looking older male who made you think, "Oooh daddy!" and, like the Rominov boys, his sons were both gorgeous males with just the right hint of bad boy about them to make any girl swoon. Dariusz was especially yummy, and if I hadn't been so head over heels in love with Marko, I would have been going all groupie on his ass.

I took a seat next to Marko at the large rectangular table, waiting for the first file to load. He projected everything onto a big screen for us all to see. We sat in silence as the first video began.

I'd always enjoyed crime thrillers and horror movies, so I thought if I treated this like fiction, I wouldn't be as badly affected. I was so wrong. A wave of nausea hit me as the horrifying scenes played out. My stomach churned and my hands grew clammy. What the heck was I doing here? Why did I feel the need to watch this?

Desperate to remain in control, I took deep, steadying breaths, exhaling slowly. I was relieved none of the other women wanted to view this. Gracie and Sonia were pregnant, so they were better off staying ignorant about the files. They knew the general idea of what these hunts entailed; we'd all discussed it, but there was a world of difference between knowing and seeing. I knew Eilidh had witnessed some pretty grim stuff as a police officer, but even she had opted out. I couldn't blame her. This stuff was horrific.

"Fuck, this is some sick shit," Ash stated, echoing my thoughts.

Miki and Glowacki both grunted their agreement, while the rest of us sat in shocked silence, eyes glued to the screen. These men were hardened criminals, capable of torturing and killing others. Yet, each one of them looked as sickened as I felt. It was oddly reassuring that they were as affected by this as I was.

Marko's family had been good to me since we met, but they were criminals. I had to admit, that thought still scared me a little. Seeing their reaction to the footage made me feel better about them. It showed me that despite their dangerous lifestyle, they had some good in them. They weren't like the MP or the twisted souls behind Darkest Desire Productions. They were predators, sure, and not to be underestimated, but they had a moral code that the men in the videos lacked.

Thank God, I thought, glancing around the room. If they had been like those other men, I'd have been doomed. Instead, they were helping to eliminate those who inflicted such horror. These men might hurt or kill, but only those they saw as credible threats. They didn't harm innocents or target women and children. They weren't on the same level as the psychopaths in these videos. In their world, they did what they had to, but managed to keep some semblance of morality. I respected and admired that. It couldn't be easy.

Screams of agony snapped me back to the screen. I watched, horrified, as a young man—barely a teenager—was torn apart by dogs while grown men laughed and jeered. I swallowed the bile rising in my throat. I didn't want to succumb to the waves of nausea, because if I did, the men would make me leave the room. In some ways, that would have been a blessing, but I knew it wasn't what I wanted. I needed to know what the MP was capable of. God, how I wished I didn't, but I did.

The next video was even worse. I shut my eyes, trying to block out the horrific images of the woman on the screen and what was happening to her, but I couldn't block out her cries of anguish. Dizziness overwhelmed me, and I felt like I might pass out. Suddenly, Marko was there, wrapping his arms around me and pulling me close. I rested my head on his shoulder as he kissed my forehead. The bodily contact was the grounding comfort I desperately needed.

"If you need to leave, we can. Or we can take a break," he whispered.

I shook my head. He knew I wanted to be here despite everything.

When Marko had finally decoded the files late last night and we planned to view them together today, the men had advised the other women against participating. When I insisted on watching, they didn't protest. This was my mission, after all.

Mathieson had dragged me into this mess, and then the MP took it further. They'd compromised my safety, destroyed my home and memories, and turned my life upside down. It was my right to see this through. My right to reclaim my life and seek revenge, even if it meant enduring scenes that made me sick.

I was relieved I had never met my biological father. My dad was the best—irreplaceable. Sure, he had stolen valuable items and occasionally gambled, but he was still a good man. Thanks to him, I'd grown up with a moral compass I might not have had if Mathieson had been in my life. I shuddered to think how different my life might have been with him around.

Mathieson wasn't truly part of *Darkest Desires*, but he knew about it, and only wanted to stop it by using me after his death. He committed plenty of crimes himself. I'd never wished for anyone's death before or been glad someone was dead, but I was glad Mathieson was gone. I wished Miki would kill the MP instead of just turning over the evidence. Anyone who could do, or allow, such horrors didn't deserve to live. In fact, I could kill him myself.

As these thoughts crossed my mind, I cringed. I didn't want to become like either of those men, but these thoughts made me wonder if I was, even just a little. Maybe Miki was right; it was best to let the authorities handle him and anyone else involved.

Marko shifted me closer to him when I sighed, and I could feel his eyes on me. I glanced up. He was watching me, his brows furrowed in concern.

"Are you sure you are okay continuing? You've seen

enough, you really don't need to watch anymore," he whispered.

I squeezed him around the waist, lifting my lips in what I hoped was at least a semblance of a smile, then nodded. I was, but only because he was here with me.

Sinking back into his embrace, tilting my head to rest on his shoulder, I continued to watch the screen in front of me.

We viewed the files for the next few hours. Every video filled me with more and more disgust and loathing for all of those involved.

The last one was the worst of all. It showed Mathieson's sister and her teenage daughter, the aunt and cousin I never met, suffering the same fate as the others. By the end, tears streamed down my face, and I sobbed in Marko's arms. All the while he sat there simply stroking my back, not saying anything, just offering me his silent support.

Once it was over, everyone seemed a bit shell-shocked.

"Fuck, and I thought binge watching the reality shows with Sonia for hours was bad. I'll never complain about that again," Romi muttered, running his fingers through his hair.

"I'll never be able to unsee that last one," Dariusz stated, shaking his head and looking sickened.

"Sorry, Melissa," Daniel mumbled, reaching over to pat me awkwardly on the knee.

"Yeah, sorry for your loss. You might not have known your aunt and cousin, but seeing them killed like that has to be fucking awful," Ash said, his voice laced with sympathy.

I nodded through watery tears.

From what Marko had told me of him, just a few weeks ago, seeing what was done to the female victims would have sent Ash over the edge, spiralling out of control in anger. Gracie had helped him get over his guilt and get more control over his emotions. He'd also gone back to counselling and this time, it seemed to have a more positive effect on him.

"We're ending that bastard now!" Glowacki stated, his voice betraying his barely contained rage.

Murmurs of agreement filled the room.

"Marko, take Melissa upstairs. We'll get everything sent to law enforcement first thing in the morning. We've done enough today," Miki said.

CHAPTER 30
MARKO
SEVERAL WEEKS LATER – DIGGING DEEPER

"'m home," Luca announced, entering my office and plonking himself down heavily into a chair.

"Love the bald head, it suits you. Makes you look your age," I smirked.

"Fuck off!" Luca said with a chuckle, throwing a marker pen at my head.

"So, the fucker's been arrested then?" he asked.

"Yeah, the joint Scotland Yard, National Crime Agency, and Interpol operation finally took place late last night. The MP and many of his staff were arrested," I confirmed.

The day after the viewing of his recorded files, I'd let Melissa press send on the anonymous email we sent to our Interpol contact. Then we had to sit tight and await the outcome.

We'd been lucky that the security guards had only seen us outside the MP's house. Between that and the fact that we had left no trace of having actually been inside, Luca told us that the MP was of the belief that our break-in had been thwarted before it could take place.

So, he had gone about his usual business without a care in the world until Interpol got their act together and organised a raid on his home. Because of the nature of the crimes involved and the fact that his operations spanned several countries, a multi-agency collaboration had been necessary and that took time to co-ordinate.

I'd been monitoring the police contacts to ensure I knew exactly when the operation was going down. Luca had also remained undercover so he could monitor the MP while we waited and ensure that the guy didn't get tipped off about a possible investigation and destroy the evidence.

As soon as I'd learned when the raid was taking place, I'd called Luca and got him out of there. He would be staying at the Estate for the foreseeable future to keep a low profile for a while. We had no doubt that once the MP was arrested, he'd figure out that enough evidence to create suspicion in law enforcement had been stolen after all and along with Luca's sudden disappearance, he would know he'd been involved and try to locate his whereabouts.

Even though Luca had changed his appearance to disguise himself and used a fake name while undercover, we wanted to ensure his hair grew back and he looked more like himself than the MP's newest bodyguard, before he went out in public again. Just to be on the safe side.

"Sonia and your staff are keeping everything running for you until you can get back to things," I told him.

Hopefully, it would be safe enough for Luca to resume his usual duties soon. I knew he was longing to get back to his role heading up our entertainment venues, but it would have to wait. We'd put him in jeopardy when he'd gone undercover for us, and we needed to ensure that it was safe for him before he resumed his normal life.

We'd also put Anton and Marcie in jeopardy when we involved them in our plans, but we crafted a scenario where Anton seemed fooled by a deceptive employee, and Marcie appeared as an innocent victim of car theft. We framed another staff member of hers to look guilty of aiding the would-be thieves and paid him to vanish afterward. Hopefully, that would prevent the MP from blaming Anton or Marcie and shield them from any backlash. All going well none of them would need to worry about the MP in the future.

"Did you take a nap?" I asked.

"Yeah, and several showers. I can't help feeling dirty, having just been in that slimy bastard's company for a few weeks," he replied with a shudder.

"Well, brace yourself, since you're stuck here for a while, you'll be helping me and Daniel Glowacki identify all the men who took part in the hunts," I told him.

"Fuck! No. I'd rather be skinned alive than watch that monster's handiwork?" he said with a look that told me he would indeed view that as a better option.

Unfortunately, I needed the help.

"Sorry, during the filming of the hunts, identities were protected by masks and the only people recognisable were the MP and his staff, so I have my work cut out for me. I really need the help or I would spare you. Daniel drew the short straw too," I told him and meant it.

If I could prevent others from witnessing that fucker's idea of entertainment, I would, but unfortunately I couldn't do this alone. Not even with Daniel's help.

Daniel Glowacki's role in the Polish Mafia was like mine, in that he was the Glowacki family's expert in computers, and would be a great asset in trying to identify all the victims.

Besides, Daniel's family was also targeted by Mathieson, and the MP was the driving force behind his actions. We knew why we were targeted by these men; our father was a party to the downfall of their father; however, we were not sure why they targeted Glowacki. It could just have been an attempt to weaken us by breaking up our alliance as we originally thought, but it seemed more personal than that, especially since the MP had continued the attacks on the Polish as well as us, although as yet we had not found another reason. But whatever it was, like us, the Glowacki's had a vested interest in bringing the guy down.

So, Glowacki had volunteered Daniel to help. Lucky Daniel!

Although the MP had kept a file on each participant, they were in code. Daniel and I had been working on it, but it was proving a hard task. Josh had been busy with other stuff but would be free to join the fun soon, and now Luca was on board. Between us all, I was confident we'd soon crack it.

Of course, it would take our law enforcement contacts a lot longer. Law enforcement or not, they just didn't have the resources we had, so once again, we would anonymously help them out.

As soon as we deciphered the code, the four of us would track down the participants. Then decide which of the bastards we'd hand over to the law, for their sorry asses to be sent to jail, and which of them we'd deal with ourselves. In one way or another, for every victim, justice would be done.

It would be some time for this whole business to be dealt with, but with the MP's arrest, at least we were now one step closer.

I checked the news. As expected, the MP's arrest was on every channel. The authorities hailed it as a great success, charging the MP and several of his men with numerous counts of murder.

Unfortunately, despite the seriousness of the charges, many of the men, including the MP, had been granted bail. As a prominent member of the British government and a wealthy man with global business interests, he wasn't considered a flight risk, apparently.

That was likely true, at least for now. He had to resign as Foreign Secretary, but he still controlled a substantial fortune and several businesses, so I doubted fleeing was in his plans. At least not quite yet.

I figured he would try to beat or at least reduce the charges first. He was an arrogant bastard and in his arrogance he would probably believe he could get out of this unscathed. The evidence was stacked against him, but money talks and I expected he would do everything to avoid prison.

Miki was convinced that until he was convicted, he remained a threat to all of us. I agreed, so I was monitoring all his communications, ready to alert the authorities if he tried anything. The media frenzy since his arrest would probably keep him virtually under house arrest, with reporters camped outside his home. That would help curtail some of his actions and hopefully stop any further attacks against us, but nevertheless, we were being extra vigilant.

The MP would likely suspect us of being behind his capture. So, for now, we needed to watch our backs.

The sooner the trial happened, and he was convicted, the better. We intended to do all we could to ensure that happened, and that he didn't decide to run after all.

Even after conviction, he could still pose a threat to us.

However, while committing his crimes, he used many petty criminals, prostitutes, drug addicts, and runaways for his "hunting" parties. These people had families, and many of his victims' loved ones wanted to see him suffer for his crimes.

As such, he would have numerous enemies when he got to prison. We intended on capitalising upon that. We would not be killing the MP in jail ourselves, but we would ensure that our contacts inside made it easier for his other enemies to do so. That way, he would receive the justice he required, but with no direct connection to the Bratva or the Polish Mafia.

We just had to bide our time.

"But you can wait to get started on things until Daniel gets here later," I told Luca.

"Go grab some time to yourself. I'm taking Melissa over to meet with Anton and the architect designing her rebuild. I'll catch up with you at dinner," I said, logging out of my system.

"Yeah, catch you later," he replied as I left the room.

Melissa was renting out her building once it was re-done to Anton. We'd finally had "the talk" a couple of days after we'd sent the info to Interpol, and she'd agree to be mine and stay here with me. I was over the moon.

Our relationship had been even stronger since we'd cleared up any concerns we'd had about our feelings for each other.

After viewing the MP's files, Melissa had been distraught. She'd needed a distraction from the awful stuff we'd seen, and I gladly provided her with one. All night long! In fact, every night since and whenever else I had the opportunity. Distracting Melissa had become a bit of an obsession for me. One that both of us were thoroughly enjoying, and I suspected we always would.

Those thoughts naturally drove me wild with need, and I decided to pass the wait, reliving some of those wonderful distractions.

CHAPTER 31
MELISSA
THE SAME DAY – FINDING MY PLACE

Carefully lifting the photographic paper out of the developing fluid, I pinned up another photograph to dry.

I was in a small basement room, which was once a large storage cupboard, now converted as my darkroom with Miki's approval. Marko had also set up a desk for me in the corner of his outer office, where Luca, Daniel, and others worked. This setup allowed me to work on my digital projects and course assignments comfortably, and my sexy Russian said he enjoyed having me nearby, which was sweet.

Working in the darkroom was amazing. While I made many digital prints, I had several old-style cameras that required film, and I loved taking photographs with them and developing the negatives. Recently, I spent a lot of time there, especially when I wasn't in college, developing photographs for my final portfolio and my very first show.

The Glowacki's were hosting several business associates and some family from Poland soon and wanted something small but interesting. An exhibition of my work was Sonia's idea, and she and Marcie were helping me plan it. Over the past few weeks, I had built a relationship with all the women in the house, getting to know them well through using them as models.

Marcie was particularly supportive, offering helpful tips on how to pose the models and suggesting interesting locations for the shoots. Sonia, being naturally glamorous, enjoyed modelling and made a great subject. Nonna, with her ageless elegance, brought a unique charm to the photographs. Using the house's beautiful grounds and various Rominov properties, especially Glitz, provided stunning and varied backdrops, making my work even more dynamic and interesting.

The entire process of preparing for the show, from shooting to developing to planning the exhibition, was a thrilling experience. The support from everyone, especially Marko, who often checked on my progress, made it even more special. With everything coming together, I felt a mix of anticipation and nervous energy, eager to showcase my work at the upcoming event.

Even Marko's stunning aunt Marta and her stepdaughter Magdalena posed for my photos, which piqued Glowacki's interest in my work. Photographing all the men would have been great, but so far, Marko was the only male model in my collection. The black-and-white prints of him in a tux had an old-school charm that I loved.

Plans for my next set of photographs included capturing everyone in black and white, inspired by Marko's photos. The idea was to photograph them in their sports cars, at their desks, and more. Also, a themed shoot, maybe from the 1930s with old-fashioned cars, seemed like it would turn out beautifully if the family could be convinced. They usually preferred to keep a low profile in the media and were rarely seen in photographs by the paparazzi, but they had intimated they would be happier being photographed by me. Especially now they had offloaded some of their criminal activities and were not as concerned with piquing the interest of reporters or law enforcement as much.

Miki had even suggested I could be the official photographer for their businesses, while Marcie mentioned hiring me for other suitable events.

My biggest highlight so far was photographing the cover for Gracie's next book. One of Anton's men posed for the "book boyfriend" cover photo, since he fitted the character's descriptions so well. Marko was a bit jealous, and insisted on watching, but it was a great shoot. Marcie's friend, a makeup artist, enjoyed oiling up the guy's body. Without my own book boyfriend, I'd have fought her for that job because, oh my gosh, phew!

Gracie, thrilled with the pictures, even paid me. That first proper photography job left me grinning when she handed me the cash. Between that, Miki's offer, and future prospects from Marcie's business, my photography business was off to a strong start. It was so exciting and kept me busy, which helped keep my mind off worrying about the MP and his pending conviction.

The MP remained a threat until convicted, which worried me. Anything happening to Marko, his family, or the Glowacki family would be awful. They had grown on me, and fitting in here had become a joy. Finding my place in life and becoming part of the family was wonderful. Loving Marko, even after only six weeks, felt right.

We had talked about things and were now officially living together. Everything happened so fast. Normally, it might have seemed too fast, but the situation thrust us together quickly. Falling for each other felt natural. Without this situation, we might never have met, so it seemed meant to be. The future together looked promising.

The only cloud on the horizon was the time we had to wait for the MP to be brought to trial. It had us all on tenterhooks. The sooner it was over, the sooner we could breathe more easily and get on with our lives. Then Marko and I had some plans to travel for a few months. We were having great fun planning where we wanted to go and what we wanted to do.

"Better than any book boyfriend?" he asked, wiggling his eyebrows, his voice filled with mirth.

My lips twitched, and I shook my head at his antics.

Marko had continued to take his challenge seriously, and every day liked to have fun with it. For such a dangerous man, he really was such a silly, sexy nerd.

"Yes, way better than any book boyfriend!" I giggled.

"Gotta keep up my reputation," he said, winking and grinning like a fool.

I continue giggling as he grabbed my hand, and we ran up the stairs.

CHAPTER 32
MARKO

When we entered the site that had once held Melissa's home, nothing remained. Only some scorched earth and a sizeable hole betrayed the fact that a building had been there and had burnt down. The demolition crew had done their job and removed all the debris. I wasn't sure how Melissa would feel being back here and seeing it empty. Glancing at her, I could see her eyes filling with unshed tears.

"Are you okay, sweetheart?" I asked, putting my arm around her. She sniffed hard and wiped at her eyes, nodding.

"It is hard to see it empty like this, but there is nothing I can do about it. Time to move on," she said, obviously trying to convince herself.

I gave her shoulder a quick squeeze and kissed her on the forehead before leading her over to where Anton was chatting with the architect.

"Melissa," I said, placing a hand on her back as we reached them, "this is Lee Wilson, the architect responsible for your new block of flats and a close friend of Ash and Anton's. Lee, this is Melissa."

Lee extended his hand with a warm smile. "Pleasure to meet you, Melissa. I've heard a lot about your vision for the new apartments."

Melissa shook his hand, her eyes sparkling with excitement. "Thank you, Lee. I can't wait to see the plans. I've been dreaming about this for days."

Anton chimed in, his voice full of enthusiasm. "Lee's the best in the business. We're lucky to have him on board and his team will also be project managing things once you sign off on the plans."

Lee nodded modestly. "I appreciate that, Anton. Melissa, I'm eager to get your input on a few key aspects of the design. Your feedback will be crucial."

Melissa nodded, glancing at me with a smile. "I'm ready. Let's make this happen."

Lee walked us through the site, explaining the layout for the new building, and then led us over to a makeshift office that had been set up to house the project manager. Once inside, he spread out the plans on a wooden table and we spent the next half hour going over them.

Melissa was thrilled with the drawings and couldn't stop oohing and aahing over them. I smiled, pleased at how excited she was at every little detail.

The new building was going to be stunning. A long rectangular three-storey grey-fronted building with floor-to-ceiling windows made of bulletproof glass. The materials used would all be flame-retardant, and the sprinkler system was top quality. Anton and I had designed the security system, which would also be top of the range.

There were three sizeable luxurious apartments, each with three bedrooms, on the upper floors. Underneath, there was an extra-large double garage and a small gym complete with an indoor pool and a training area.

Anton was extremely happy with the design; the gym and training room were an especially big hit with him. He was renting all the apartments, planning on using one for himself and renting the other for some of his security staff to use when needed.

Melissa was not only over the moon with the plans but especially happy to have ready-made tenants too. I was really pleased for her because although we were now officially living together, and I was more than happy to take care of her, I knew she needed to retain her independence.

This apartment building would give her one source of income, and the photography business she was setting up would provide another.

My Little Miss Pouty Lips had decided not to use the money Mathieson had left her. Instead, she had given it to me to keep in trust. When we discovered the families of those people murdered in the MP's hunts, we were going to ensure that they each received sizeable sums. Of course, we couldn't just hand it to them directly. However, they would suddenly find themselves beneficiaries of wills from previously unknown relatives, or lottery and other prize winners.

Watching her gushing with enthusiasm over the design of the pool, I couldn't help but smile. Her excitement lit up her face and my heart clenched. Melissa was stunning and I couldn't have been more proud of how much she had dealt with and everything she had achieved in just a few months since losing her dad.

Melissa signed her name on the papers with a flourish. "Yey!" she squealed, clapping her hands excitedly when she'd done so.

The plans were finished with only minor changes being made to the size of the gym and training spaces, and the addition of a large carport at the back of the house where Anton could keep extra security vehicles.

Seeing the plans for the new building had cured Melissa's upset, especially as Lee had made it a priority to retain as much of the original garden and the rosebush planted in memory of her mum, and she was practically buzzing with excitement as we said goodbye to him.

As we left the site, Anton and I chatted about one of his current jobs where he had men acting as bodyguards to an Instagram influencer. I was so busy laughing at some of the antics he told me his men had endured while working for the woman that I didn't take proper notice of my surroundings, a mistake I regretted later.

Melissa was walking just slightly behind us as we left the grounds because the pavement was not wide enough for all three of us to walk side by side, but it was not far enough behind for me to be worried. Another mistake I would regret later!

A jogger came towards us. His outfit and demeanour were that of a young nondescript man, out for a morning jog, listening to his music. There were no red flags, so I didn't feel any danger until it was too late. As the jogger passed, he didn't even look in our direction. He simply veered onto the road for a few steps until he passed us, then swerved back onto the pavement immediately after. That's when my hackles rose, and I knew something was wrong.

Anton must have felt it too as we both turned quickly, just in time to see him collide with Melissa and hear an "Oof!" from her before she doubled over. She reached for her side and pulled her hand away, and there was blood.

My world stopped for a heartbeat as my own blood drained from my face. I rushed to her, lifting her up and shouting for Trigger, who was waiting by the car. Anton took off after the jogger, who was now sprinting away. Trigger and I got Melissa into the car; she seemed dazed, and I feared she might go into shock.

Trigger sped towards the Estate, weaving through the late morning traffic, and throwing frantic glances at us through the rear-view mirror.

My mind raced with worry and fury—furious with myself for letting her get hurt and enraged at the bastard who'd done this. I was ready to kill him. Anton had better catch the fucker; he couldn't get away. Shaking with nerves and rage, I tore off my shirt, sat Melissa on my lap, and pressed the shirt against her wound while dialling Miki.

After filling Miki in and getting his promise that our doctor would be waiting for us, I finally took the time to examine Melissa's side properly.

"I need to have a look," I said, easing her hand away and lifting her T-shirt up. She cried out when I moved her, and my heart clenched. I hated that she was in pain.

"I'm sorry, sweetheart. I know it hurts, but you're going to be fine."

Thankfully, the stab wound didn't look as bad as it had first seemed. I took a deep, shuddering breath and released it slowly, trying to calm my racing heart. I sniffed hard, the gravity of it hitting me—she could have been killed. Instead, she'd probably need a few stitches and be sore for a while, but she would heal. Thank god.

"The doctor will be waiting when we get home, and he'll fix you up," I told her, trying to keep my voice even so she couldn't tell how close I was to losing my shit.

Taking another deep breath, I reminded myself that it was just a shallow wound which would only have caused minimal damage. But that did nothing to assuage my anger.

That someone dared to attack my woman made my blood boil. This had to be the MP's doing, and I made a mental note to ensure that when the time came, he suffered in jail before he was finally killed.

The jogger who stabbed her wouldn't escape my wrath either. I hoped Anton would catch the bastard, but if not,

I'd track him down myself. When I was done, he wouldn't be attacking any more women.

Hugging her close, I kissed Melissa's forehead, noticing that her eyes were heavy and her skin pale. I feared she was going into shock. Seeing the Estate come into view was a relief. As we drove along the long driveway, Anton called with bad news—he hadn't caught the jogger. My frustration at his escape boiled beneath the surface; knowing that bastard was still out there, free and untouched, stoked my anger even more, but I bit down hard on my fury, pushing it aside to focus on my woman.

I carried a barely conscious Melissa into the house and straight to our small makeshift hospital room, where Doctor Rawlins was waiting.

"Get her up onto the bed," he told me, and I quickly followed his instructions.

Doctor Rawlins had been our family doctor since we moved from Russia. Though British, he had once been threatened by a rogue group of Albanians who kidnapped his daughter to coerce him into providing drugs through his practice. My dad handled the situation and returned the girl unharmed. In gratitude, the doctor had helped us ever since with discreet medical issues. Dad always compensated him well, and they grew to be good friends. We trusted him with our lives.

The doctor handled Melissa gently, his hands steady as he cut off her T-shirt and cleaned her wound. After assessing the injury, he looked at me with a reassuring nod.

"It's not as serious as it might have been," he told her, his voice calm.

Melissa's eyes fluttered open. Lifting her bag, the doctor showed us a hole in the leather.

"It looks like the knife penetrated your bag first, which reduced the force of the attack and kept the injury from being deeper. You're quite lucky. The wound is shallow— just a few stitches will do," he told her.

Melissa nodded, relief evident in her strained expression.

"I'm going to give you a local anaesthetic and we'll get you patched up," Doctor Rawlins said gently, preparing to tend to her stitches.

Holding her hand, I said softly, "Relax sweetheart, I'm here and the doc will take good care of you."

Melissa's eyes fluttered shut again, and she sighed as I stroked her hair with my free hand.

A short while later, the doc was finished closing her up.

"That's you all sorted. Take these and then you can rest and I will be back to check you over in a couple of days," he said, giving her some painkillers.

Withing minutes of her swallowing them and lying back on the bed, she was out like a light.

"Thanks, Doc," I said as he waved goodbye and left.

CHAPTER 33
MELISSA
A FEW WEEKS LATER – THE PHOTOGRAPHIC SHOW

I
t had been a few weeks since I was stabbed, and I was healing well, having only required a few stitches. My favourite tote bag had saved me from further harm, sacrificing itself in the process. I was so glad I had brought my camera to the site that day to take some pictures and had put it into my bag as I left; in doing so, I may just have saved myself.

The whole ordeal left me seething. Another attempt on my life, and it didn't take a genius to know the MP was behind it. Marko was furious, too. He ramped up my security to the point where I couldn't step outside without a shadow. If he had his way, I'd never leave the house. He tried to put me under what felt like house arrest again, all in the name of safety. But I refused to be a prisoner in my own home. We all faced danger, but I wouldn't let the MP, Marko, or anyone else control my life. I had a life to live, and I intended to live it fully.

Nevertheless, Trigger was my constant shadow now, and I was grateful to him. His presence was both a comfort and a reminder of the dangers lurking. He even accompanied me to college lectures. At first, the lecturers were uneasy about his presence, but after Marko had a chat with the head of the college—and made a substantial donation—there were no more issues. Money talks, and in this case, it spoke volumes. Not that his presence would be a problem for much longer anyway, as I was nearly finished the course.

The MP was finally due in court in a few days, and with any luck, he'd plead guilty and bring this ordeal to a swift conclusion and this whole nightmare Mathieson had dragged me into would be over.

Thankfully, there had been no further attacks against the Rominov family or businesses, but Glowacki hadn't been as fortunate. Though we lacked direct proof, we believed the MP was involved. Who else would it be, after all?

Someone had tried to run over Sebastian and Magdalena, Janusz Glowacki's youngest children, but their alert security prevented any harm. Glowacki was livid, and I couldn't blame him. Only monsters would target kids.

While Glowacki's children had thankfully survived the attempt on their lives, some of his men were not so fortunate.

Two of his men were killed when one of their drug shipments was targeted and the truck was stolen. Another was on a supply run between dealers when he was murdered. And there had been an incident with one of his restaurants, which was shut down for a week due to a sudden influx of cockroaches—clearly sabotage—which had a detrimental effect on the business, though was quickly resolved.

Thankfully, the restaurant hosting my photographic show hadn't been targeted. I was happy about that because tonight was the big night, and I was anxious as hell as I stood beside Marko and Vlad and pretended to listen while they talked.

My hands shook, my mind a whirlwind of concern, and my emotions felt like they were on a rollercoaster. One minute, I was elated, convinced everything would go smoothly. The next, I feared something would go wrong, and my photographs would flop.

Feeling fidgety, I checked my reflection in the tall wall mirror for the hundredth time. I wore a gorgeous black lace bodycon dress designed by Marcie's friend Sara. It was stunning and despite my nerves, I felt beautiful, elegant, and sophisticated in it.

Sara's up-and-coming label, *'Simply Sara'*, was taking London by storm, and I felt lucky to be wearing one of her originals. It was even more thrilling that she had asked me to photograph her collection for her buyers.

Sara was a stunning woman in her early thirties who had worked for a major fashion label before striking out on her own. Funny and always impeccably dressed, we hit it off immediately. I couldn't wait to work with her. I also noticed how she blushed and got flustered whenever she looked at Trigger. Trigger, in turn, couldn't take his eyes off her whenever we visited to discuss my dress.

I'd deliberately sent Trigger to collect my dress the other day with the hint that he should ask Sara out. From the secret smile he wore when he handed me the dress later that day, I thought he might have, but so far he was keeping quiet about it. Naturally, I had asked, but he just smirked, winked and declined to answer. The infuriating bugger!

Was I matchmaking? Absolutely!

And why not? I really liked Trigger. We had become friends, and I enjoyed his company. He had even shown an interest in my photography, helping me set up the lighting and giving his opinion on my shots. I found he had a great eye for detail and was technical—qualities that made him a great sniper, I supposed.

Marko had told me that Trigger used to suffer from PTSD, but after a lot of therapy, he seemed to have that under control now. He was genuinely such a decent guy, despite his role within the Bratva, so it would be nice if he could find someone. I really hoped that someone would be Sara.

Movement caught my eye, and I saw Glowacki nodding my way. Oh no. He had been schmoozing with his family members and business associates for the last hour, but now it was time to officially open my show. My steps felt sluggish as I moved to stand near him.

My palms were sweating, and I suddenly felt claustrophobic. It was my turn to speak next, and dread gnawed at me. I had been rehearsing my short speech in my head all day, and it was driving me nuts. I just wanted to get this over with and enjoy the rest of the night.

Glowacki called everyone to attention and gave a short speech, thanking them for coming.

Oh god. I was so nervous I thought I might be sick. I hated giving speeches and being the centre of attention. Shifting from side to side, I tried not to make it noticeable. I couldn't stand still; I was so jittery. Heck, I was going to pee.

'Cool and calm, Melissa, cool and calm,' I told myself, taking a deep breath as Glowacki introduced me and I took to the small makeshift stage.

It wasn't working. My whole body started to shake. I didn't think I could do this. I looked at the audience and gulped, my breath hitching. A slight movement caught my eye as Marko moved into my line of vision and smiled. He gave me a small nod and mouthed, "you've got this!" In that instance, the breath I'd been holding released in a whoosh, and I calmed down.

Marko was right. With him as my biggest fan, I had indeed got this. I smiled back, opened my mouth, and let the words flow.

CHAPTER 34
MARKO
THE SAME NIGHT – THE PLANNED
SURPRISE

My chest puffed with pride as I watched Melissa mill around the room like a pro. I could hardly believe that such a stunningly beautiful, talented woman was mine. After her shaky start, she was really coming into her own. When she finished her short speech, I had clapped and whistled loudly, making her blush a little as she grinned, before heading off with some guests to show them her work.

Little Miss Pouty Lips had been so nervous, but she nailed it. I was incredibly proud of her achievements over the last few weeks. Her photography business wasn't just up and running, but already going from strength to strength.

My gaze was drawn to my sexy little cat burglar as she moved among the guests and I wanted to tag along after her, but I held back. This was her night, and while I was there to back her up and encourage her, she needed to know she could own it all by herself. If she was to work through her nerves and build her confidence, she really didn't need me as her constant shadow. Instead, I contented myself with watching from a distance.

Besides, I had enough nerves of my own rearing their ugly head. I didn't want her to pick up on them and think it was a lack of confidence in her when it was entirely the opposite. My nerves were down to the surprise I had in store.

So, I stayed away and stood with Miki and Eilidh, pretending to listen to their chat. Miki had proposed to her the day we sent the information we had on the MP off to our police contacts, so now they were busy making plans for the big day.

If all went well tonight, it could mean another double wedding. That thought made my mouth suddenly as dry as dust, and I gulped down the rest of my drink. My insides churned, and I felt as jittery as a cat on a hot tin roof. I couldn't remember the last time I'd felt such a wild mix of fear and excitement.

Normally, I stayed calm under pressure, but tonight was different. I needed something to distract myself, so I slid my empty glass of champagne onto a passing waiter's tray and grabbed another. As I lifted it to my lips, I saw my hand tremble slightly. Shit, I needed to pull myself together. If I didn't, my planned surprise might end up a disaster.

"It'll be fine," I told myself, taking a few deep breaths and another sip of champagne for courage.

Miki and Eilidh began smooching and not wanting to feel like a third wheel, I slipped off and took a wander around the room. Melissa's tinkling laugh drew my notice, and I glanced over to find her laughing at something an elderly gentleman was saying as she put a red sticker against a lovely photograph of Glowacki's daughter, Magdalena. The elderly couple she was talking to must have bought it.

I checked her other photographs. She was doing well; there were quite a few red stickers on her displayed work. The night was turning out to be a great success. I hoped my surprise only added to that.

Checking my watch, I realised the main part of the night was nearly over. Not long now!

Once again Melissa laughed loudly at something, and I couldn't help smiling. I wanted to hear her laughing like that for the rest of my life—and hers.

I frowned, the memory of how close I came to losing her still sharp in my mind. The fact that someone had stabbed her while she was with me seemed unreal. My anger and frustration with myself were overwhelming, knowing I had let such a thing happen.

Weeks after the attack, I was still hunting the jogger. We knew who he was—the son of a key player in the MP's illicit operations—but he had vanished. The uncertainty of his whereabouts gnawed at me. I was determined to find him, and when I did, he'd face a reckoning.

Fortunately, there had been no further attacks on Melissa, my family, or our businesses. I had wanted to confine her to the Estate until after the MP's trial, but she refused. So, whenever she had to go out, either I or Trigger was by her side. I worried she might grow tired of Trigger's quiet, moody demeanour, but she seemed to adore him. He had even taken a shine to her as well, often saying she was good for me—which was true.

Of course, I also had several of our guys trailing her covertly. There was no way I was letting anything happen to her again.

I narrowed my eyes, lost in thought. We'd been fortunate not to face any new attacks, but Glowacki wasn't as lucky. It bothered us all that we still didn't know what the true reason for the attacks against him was, but it was becoming more evident with each attack that he was being targeted for something more than simply being our ally.

We had been monitoring all communications from the MP's home and keeping tabs on his movements. Since his arrest, he had become a virtual recluse, with the press camped outside his estate. However, for these attacks to be taking place, either some of his men based at his home were getting out undetected by the reporters, or he had more men on the outside doing his dirty work for him.

Whoever the culprits were, we needed to put a stop to them soon, because now Glowacki's youngest children were being targeted. My fists clenched in fury at the thought. According to our code, such attacks were unforgivable, and by breaking the code, the perpetrators had signed their own death warrants.

Sniggering pulled me from my thoughts and I turned to

see Miki, Ash, Romi, Luca, and Anton approaching. Their smug grins told me that the plan for tonight's surprise that I shared with Miki in confidence was no longer a secret. The fucker had obviously let all of my Bratva Blood Brothers in on it, and now I was about to get tormented. Oh, great!

"So, how are the nerves?" Miki asked, grinning from ear to ear.

"What nerves?" I countered, clearing my throat and taking a deliberate sip of champagne, feigning calm.

The guys erupted in laughter, and Luca gave me a hearty slap on the back, almost making me choke.

"Glad it's you and not me. I'd be terrified," he said, still chuckling.

"Wait until it is your turn. I want a ringside seat," Anton added with a wicked laugh.

"Ditto, Anton!" Luca shot back, and Anton's face turned a shade paler.

"Not me. I'll leave the relationship stuff to you guys," Anton said, gulping his drink in one go.

I'd always wondered why Anton shied away from long-term relationships. Since his return from the military, he'd only had one-night stands or fleeting affairs—never anything lasting. There was clearly a story there. But he was a private guy, so I'd never pried.

Anton turned away from us, then spun back around and smirked, "Maybe Trigger will be the next to pop the question."

We all looked over and noticed Trigger standing very

close to a laughing Sara. From the looks of things, he might be right. It seemed Melissa was correct that Trigger had taken a liking to Sara and from where I was standing, it very much looked like the feeling was mutual. I hoped so. The guy deserved love.

As the event was nearing the end, and the people who had been swarming around Melissa all night dwindled back into the main restaurant, I could finally approach her again.

"Your first show has gone really well. I'm so proud of you." I told her, kissing her lightly on the cheek before whispering, "and I'm looking forward to getting you home and showing you just how much."

She shivered, and I smirked, thinking of all the delightfully naughty things I had planned for when we were finally alone.

"When can we leave?" she asked, grinning, and I almost whisked her away then and there. But I had something important to do first, so instead, I pulled her to me and kissed her briefly on the lips.

"Soon. The night is nearly over, but before it is, I have something I need to do," I told her, leading her into the main restaurant.

This was it! I gave a nod to the musicians, and the string quartet began an old Russian tune, a favourite of my parents. Taking a deep breath, I dropped to one knee and pulled a small box from my pocket and opened it.

Melissa's eyes widened, and her hand flew to her mouth in shock and anticipation.

"Melissa Martin, it hasn't been long since we met, but from the moment I saw you, I knew you were special. That you were meant to be mine. I love you and want to spend the rest of my life with you, and I hope you feel the same. Will you marry me?"

Please say yes! Please say yes! My heart pounded so loudly I was sure everyone could hear it. Cold sweat beaded on my forehead as I awaited her response. The few seconds it took for her to process my words felt like an eternity.

"Yes!" she cried, and as I stood, she threw herself into my arms.

Thank fuck for that!

The room erupted in cheers, claps, and whistles, but I barely noticed. My focus was on steadying my trembling hands as I slid the ring onto her finger.

Once it was in place, a wave of relief washed over me, and I couldn't contain the beaming grin as I looked at the ring on Melissa's hand. She was mine!

Naturally, Miki was the first to congratulate us, giving me a hearty pat on the back and planting a kiss on Melissa's cheek. Glowacki followed, grinning ear to ear, with Aunt Marta beside him, glowing with joy. Their arranged marriage seemed to be working wonders; they looked blissfully happy, and I hoped Melissa and I would find the same happiness.

"Congratulazioni, figli miei," Nonna said, grasping us in turn and kissing us soundly on both cheeks, tears of joy welling up in her eyes. Her smile was enormous, a rare sight since my parents' death and Krissa's loss. But with the new additions to the family and the prospect of babies on the horizon, Nonna had a new spark. It was heartwarming to see her so rejuvenated.

After the family's congratulations, Luca, and Anton gave their well-wishes before Trigger approached. His usual moody demeanour was replaced by a rare, genuine grin. I knew he was happy for us, but I suspected his smile had more to do with the woman at his side. Sara was equally radiant, and I glanced between them, pleased that Melissa's matchmaking seemed to have worked.

We chatted briefly, and I complimented Sara on the stunning dress she'd designed for Melissa. She mentioned she'd be wearing the same dress in blue for her friend's wedding that weekend and had invited Hugh, hoping I'd give him the evening off.

I stared at her, my mind racing to connect the dots— Hugh Scott, aka Trigger!

"Ha, Hugh!" I burst out laughing, and he nudged me playfully. I had completely forgotten that was his real name. He loathed Hugh, but the fact that he let Sara use it told me he was smitten.

Smirking at him, I turned to face Sara. "He can have the whole bloody weekend off if it keeps a smile on the moody bastard's face," I told her with a wink.

Holding Melissa close at my side, I watched as they beamed at each other when I confirmed he'd be free. There was definitely a budding romance there, and I was truly happy for Trigger. If anyone deserved some joy in his life, he did.

Eventually, we headed back to the Estate, and I spent the next few hours showing my little Miss Pouty Lips just how much she meant to me. It had been a fantastic day and an even better evening. I drifted off with a giant grin on my face and a contented woman in my arms.

CHAPTER 35
MELISSA
THE FOLLOWING WEEK – MARCIE'S PARTY

Each time I glanced at my engagement ring, a rush of disbelief and joy hit me. Even a week after Marko's proposal, the sight of it still sent my heart racing, a constant reminder of how perfectly our whirlwind romance had aligned.

I looked over at Marko, deep in conversation with Miki and Romi. We were at Glitz, their new London nightclub, celebrating Marcie's 29th birthday. The VIP area was ours for the night, and the party was in full swing with everyone who mattered—except Luca. He was MIA, and the guys were starting to worry. He'd texted earlier saying he needed to grab something from his apartment, but we hadn't heard from him since. Still, Luca could take care of himself, so I expected he would turn up soon.

Claire handed me another glass of bubbly, and we laughed at Marcie, who was dancing on the table after one too many drinks. Gracie, Sonia, and Eilidh eyed our champagne glasses with longing. Eilidh was just newly pregnant, but the other two were further along, and alcohol was out for all three.

I eyed their bellies, a secret smile tugging at my lips. Though I was on contraception and not ready for a baby just yet, Marko and I had talked about it. We planned to marry in the next few months then finally go travelling for a couple of months for our honeymoon. I longed for a baby, but not yet; I wanted to enjoy some alone time with Marko first. We had adventures to go on before we started a family.

Loud, out of tune singing brought my thoughts back to the party and my gaze shifted back to Marcie, who was screeching at the top of her lungs, the words to "Wannabe" by the Spice Girls.

Wincing, I clutched my ears as her screams of "Tell me what you want, what you really, really want," threatened to burst my eardrums. God, she was awful! But I had to admire her spirit. Marcie was certainly going for it, determined to make the most of her night. Her best friend, and Gracie's cousin Claire, was up there beside her, giving it everything, singing, and giggling right along with her. That surprised me because I'd heard that Claire, who was apparently an up-and-coming defence lawyer was known as the "Ice Queen" and a bit of a ball-breaker at work. I hadn't expected her to have such a fun side.

The DJ played another song, and Eilidh joined Marcie and Claire on the table. Miki, looking worried, took up position behind her as the three women danced wildly on one of the table. I noticed that Anton was staying close to Marcie too, as he had most of the night and anytime I saw them together. I had asked Marko if there was something going on there and he said no. He told me that Marcie had a crush on Anton, but it wasn't reciprocated. However, with the way Anton watched, I wasn't sure that was true.

Pursing my lips, I wondered if I should step in and do something about the situation. After all, my match making seemed to be working for Trigger. Maybe I could take it up as another hobby.

"Not joining them?" Marko shouted in my ear over the noise as he grabbed hold of me from behind.

"I don't think any more people can safely fit on that table. And have you seen the way they are flinging their arms around? One of them is likely to fall off any minute." I laughed, all thoughts of matchmaking fleeing as he nibbled on my neck.

Just as I said that Marcie went flying backwards, but luckily Anton was there to catch her.

"Alright, birthday girl, time to quit dancing on tables!" he said, easing her down into a seat. Plopping down next to her, he handed her a glass of water. "Drink!" he told her with a disapproving shake of his head.

Marko pulled me aside. "I need you," he said as he dragged me through a staff door and into a small storage cupboard where he proceeded to show me just how much.

When we finally emerged from the cupboard, Marcie was clinging to Anton, trying to sway with him in a clumsy attempt at a slow dance. She was clearly plastered, struggling to stay upright while Anton looked like he was bracing for impact. It was obvious she needed to go home.

Without missing a beat, Anton grabbed her bag and jacket. "Alright, birthday girl, time to head home," he said, guiding her into a seat and draping her jacket over her shoulders. Claire tried to mask her amusement behind her glass, clearly entertained by the scene.

Marcie gave her best pout, then promptly threw up all over herself before passing out. Anton just shook his head, a resigned smile on his lips. "I'll take her home," he said, scooping her up with surprising ease.

CHAPTER 36
MARKO

A grin spread across my face as I watched Anton carry an inebriated Marcie, bride style, out of the club. His pretence of indifference was transparent—everyone could see he was just as smitten with her as she was with him.

The dynamics between them were baffling; Marcie was charismatic and gorgeous, with a personality that shone brightly. Yet, despite their mutual attraction, Anton resisted a relationship. I overheard Marcie confiding in Claire about her frustration with his mixed signals. She had tried dating others, only to have Anton show up and disrupt her plans each time.

It was clear he had feelings but also deep-seated issues with commitment. He needed to make a decision —either commit to Marcie or step back so she could move on. All of us guys had tried to talk to him about it in the past, but no matter what we said, the guy wouldn't discuss it and continued to profess his feelings for her were merely platonic. Which was glaringly untrue.

I had a feeling that it would take something big to happen before he would face things. The thought was concerning, but in the end it was really none of my business.

Despite the obvious problems between the pair, it had been a great night, and Marcie had obviously thoroughly enjoyed herself. She had been in great form this evening, but I doubted she would be feeling quite as great in the morning. That girl was in for one hell of a hangover!

Laughter erupted from my brothers, and I glanced their way. Claire fought to keep her composure but soon dissolved into peals of laughter at whatever Ash had said. Gracie quickly joined in, and the room buzzed with infectious joy that had both Melissa and I grinning too.

Melissa's laugh bubbled up as she said, "Claire's really letting loose tonight. I thought you said she was a ball-breaker and a bit uptight?"

"She is, but everyone has their moments," I replied, chuckling. "It's nice to see her thawing out for once."

From across the room, Sonia's voice rang out, "Stop, I'm about to pee my pants!" Ash cracked another joke, and Miki's laughter rolled over us while Eilidh giggled uncontrollably.

Watching them all in such high spirits warmed my heart. Claire, the Ice Queen, was finally showing a softer side. Known for her steely lawyer persona and intimidating reputation, it was a great to see her laugh and relax.

Thinking about Claire made my thoughts turn to Luca, and I scanned the crowd for him. Like Marcie had a crush on Anton, I knew that Luca had a thing for Claire. He was also close with Marcie, and had been looking forward to her party and a chance to spend some time with Claire. So where was he? I couldn't see him anywhere. In fact, the more I thought about it the more I realised I hadn't seen him all night. That was odd.

Hadn't he turned up? Or had I missed him?

Luca had been staying at his room in the Estate with us but had left earlier to pick up Marcie's birthday gift from his apartment in the city centre, but that shouldn't have taken him long.

Shit. Something was off. A sense of dread hit me. I could be wrong, but I had a strong sense that something bad had happened. As Melissa chatted with some of Marcie's friends, I whispered to her that I'd be right back, then headed off to find Miki.

"Have you seen Luca?" I asked, pulling him aside.

"No," he replied, shaking his head. "In fact, I haven't seen him all night," he said, suddenly looking worried.

Shit. I scratched my head, my sense of dread building. Why wasn't he here?

"Check with the others and see if anyone knows where he is. I'll try his tracker," I told Miki as I opened my phone to do just that.

"He's at his apartment," I said a few seconds later.

Frowning, Miki nodded and called Luca.

"No answer," he said before typing up a message.

"I've told him to call me. He was only supposed to be going to his apartment to collect Marcie's present, he shouldn't still be there," Miki said, the concern clear in his voice.

Our tension mounted as several minutes passed, and there was no response to Miki's message.

Miki sent Trigger off to Luca's flat to check on him before trying Luca's phone again.

"Still no answer," he said.

It went straight to voicemail, "Luca, where the fuck are you? We're worried. Call me the fuck back!" Miki barked, worry making way to anger.

Minutes passed and there was still no word.

Miki was Luca's best friend, but he was also our Pakhan, so when he told you to call him, you called. For Luca to not call back immediately was highly unusual. The longer he went without getting in touch, the more we knew something had happened. Something bad.

The night was coming to a close and most people had left, leaving only our family, Glowacki's and a few stragglers remaining.

We rejoined the others and downplayed our worry as best we could while we continued to chat with everyone else, but after a further twenty minutes with no news from either Luca or Trigger, we knew we had a problem.

Leaving the women blissfully ignorant, us guys moved nearer the door to make another call.

I could feel the tension coming off Miki in waves as he tried Luca's mobile again. Once again, it went straight to voicemail. He left another curt message before ringing Trigger. His phone was still ringing when Trigger ran up to us.

"Luca's been arrested!" he said. Stunned silence greeted the comment.

Well, shit!

Trigger gave us a brief rundown of the situation. Luca had been arrested for the rape and murder of a young woman in his flat.

"Bollocks!" Ash screamed.

"There's no fucking way Luca would do anything like that," I said.

"It's obviously nonsense. He's been set up," Miki stated, "Now we know why the MP hasn't attacked anyone for the last week. He hasn't been too busy dealing with his own court case as we'd thought; he's been busy plotting revenge against Luca."

Fuck!

Miki narrowed his eyes and his voice betrayed his barely contained fury, "Romi, grab some of our guys and take our women home. Marko, Ash. You two are coming to the police station with me."

As we kissed our women goodbye, it was hard not to notice the significant change in the atmosphere. We'd gone from high to low in the blink of an eye.

With grim resolve, we stepped into the night, our mission clear: uncover the truth and free Luca.

EPILOGUE

MARKO

SEVERAL MONTHS LATER

"Hurry up!" Melissa cried, tugging impatiently on my hand as she practically dragged me toward the hospital wing.

"Slow down, sweetheart. They're not going anywhere," I laughed, amused by her eagerness to see the newest members of the Rominov family. The twins had finally arrived, and Ash had texted everyone that it was time for a visit.

By the time we arrived, the rest of the family was already there, and we had to wait our turn as the nurse allowed only a few visitors at a time. While we waited, I watched Melissa giggle and chat animatedly with the other women. Despite the shadow of Luca's arrest and the recent turbulent years, this moment felt like a small beam of light in an otherwise dark period.

Sonia and Romi emerged from the room, signalling it was our turn.

"Yay!" Melissa practically jumped with giddiness, grabbing my hand and hurrying us inside.

Gracie sat up in bed, looking radiant, while Ash beamed with pride, each of them holding a baby.

"Oh my god, you've each got a mini me!" Melissa exclaimed with an excited giggle.

"Sonia said the same thing!" Ash laughed.

I had to agree; they were beautiful babies—a daughter with her mother's colouring and a son with his dad's. So sweet.

"Can I hold one?" Melissa asked.

"Of course," Ash replied, gently handing over his son.

"Oh my god, he is so adorable," Melissa cooed, staring down at the tiny bundle in her arms.

"What about you, Marko? Want to hold your niece?" Gracie asked.

"Absolutely!" I beamed, taking my niece into my arms. She seemed so small and vulnerable, and I felt a strong sense of protection wash over me.

Looking at Melissa holding my nephew, I vowed that these children would always be loved and protected. After Melissa had oohed and aahed over our nephew, we swapped so she could do the same with our niece.

"Oh, look at you; you are a beauty," Melissa cooed to the baby, and my heart clenched. She looked so natural holding a baby, and I felt a pang of longing. One day, I hoped to see her holding our child. But not yet; we had a few adventures to embark on first.

My nephew started to cry, and I passed him back to his mum. Watching him settle into her embrace, I naturally thought about how to ensure their safety when both babies began to cry.

"Time to feed them," Gracie said. After kissing the babies' foreheads, we said our goodbyes and left the new family to it.

Contentment filled me as Melissa and I walked back to the car, hand in hand, listening to her chat about the babies. I wished we could always feel this happy. Unfortunately, with both the MP's trial and Luca's still pending, that seemed unlikely. However, both were due soon, and with the mounting evidence against the MP, it was improbable he'd escape a lengthy prison sentence. Claire was working tirelessly to free Luca. If anyone could do it, she could. That woman was a force to be reckoned with!

A few months from now, I prayed our problems would be resolved, the MP eliminated, and Luca freed. Then, maybe, the dream of a life filled with family and happiness would become a reality.

In the meantime, I could enjoy moments like these. With that thought, I pulled Melissa to me and kissed her hard before heading out of the hospital.

As we drove away, I glanced at my gorgeous fiancée. "You looked even more beautiful than usual with a baby in your arms, sweetheart," I told her.

"I know we don't want to make one ourselves quite yet, but these things take practice, anyway. What do you say? Fancy some practice?" I whispered in her ear, sending shivers of pleasure through her body and igniting my own desire.

Melissa's eyes lit up mischievously, and she giggled. "Practice, huh? Well, you do have a *better than any book boyfriend* reputation to keep up!"

"Oh, I do indeed, and there's no time like the present," I said, driving toward a nearby hotel. I had already booked a room and set up a surprise. My body practically vibrated with need, imagining all the things I planned to do with her. Our life might be full of danger, but I would always ensure it was filled with passion, too.

MELISSA

"Where are we going?" I asked Marko as we pulled into a parking spot outside a hotel.

Startled, I squealed as Marko literally swept me off my feet, carrying me past the reception desk and into an awaiting lift.

When it re-opened he practically ran us down a hall, fumbling with the keycard with me still held tightly in his arms.

"What are you doing?" I asked, laughing hard at his eagerness.

"Practicing!" he grinned, tossing me onto the bed.

God, my Mr Sexy Nerd made my heart flutter. Watching him strip off, butterflies erupted in my stomach, and my core clenched with need. Life with my Bratva Hacker was dangerous and not what I had expected I would want, but it proved to be exactly what I needed. I had thought I wanted a quiet life, but with a new career as a landlady and photographer, a wedding to plan, and a Sexy Nerd to keep happy, I knew that danger, fun, and excitement suited me more.

Seeing Gracie and Ash with the twins had brought home to me how much I longed to have children of my own one day, too. It wasn't quite our time yet, but Marko was right—that didn't stop us from practicing.

Of course, I doubted we could get any better together, but if he was up for the challenge, so was I!

"Bring it on, Mr Sexy Nerd! After all, practice makes perfect!"

ABOUT THE AUTHOR

Jax Knight is a fledgling author who finally gave in to the voices in her head, letting them come to life in her first dark contemporary romance series.

Jax lives in Scotland with her husband and son. She enjoys martial arts, reading and coffee and can often be found hiding away in a corner, glued to her Kindle or with her head buried in a book while sipping a Mocha.

A sucker for sexy, protective villains with morals and feisty, fun females, all her books have them aplenty and a guaranteed happy-ever-after!

Ash is her debut novel and the first of six books in her Bratva Blood Brothers Series.

If you'd like to keep up with all of her new releases and more, please come and join her newsletter or follow her on social media to stay up to date!

ALSO BY JAX KNIGHT

Bratva Blood Brothers

Ash

Romi

Miki

Marko

Luca

Anton